Titles by MaryJanice Davidson

UNDEAD AND UNWED
UNDEAD AND UNEMPLOYED
UNDEAD AND UNAPPRECIATED
UNDEAD AND UNRETURNABLE
UNDEAD AND UNPOPULAR
UNDEAD AND UNEASY

DERIK'S BANE
SLEEPING WITH THE FISHES
SWIMMING WITHOUT A NET

Anthologies

CRAVINGS
(with Laurell K. Hamilton, Rebecca York, Eileen Wilks)

BITE
(with Laurell K. Hamilton, Charlaine Harris, Angela Knight,
Vickie Taylor)

DEAD AND LOVING IT

MYSTERIA
(with P. C. Cast, Gena Showalter, Susan Grant)

DEMON'S DELIGHT
(with Emma Holly, Vickie Taylor, Catherine Spangler)

BERKLEY JAM titles
by MaryJanice Davidson and Anthony Alongi

JENNIFER SCALES AND THE ANCIENT FURNACE
JENNIFER SCALES AND THE MESSENGER OF LIGHT
THE SILVER MOON ELM: A JENNIFER SCALES NOVEL

Praise for
Sleeping with the Fishes

"Ms. Davidson has created another laugh-out-loud, unique paranormal romance series that is bound to take off . . . *Sleeping with the Fishes* has the unique Davidson comic flair that readers have come to love . . . Among the many paranormal romances on the bookshelves, *Sleeping with the Fishes* is a 'school' apart!" —*The Romance Readers Connection*

"A zany, amusing fantasy as MaryJanice Davidson provides her trademark wacky, fun tale of the tail . . . Readers will enjoy this delightful, whimsical story." —*The Best Reviews*

"Davidson certainly knows how to capture the reader's attention . . . a hilarious romp with a mermaid, a merman, and a human with a Ph.D. that will have you rolling on the floor in laughter . . . funny with a side of danger all rolled into one neat little package." —*Romance Reviews Today*

"Known for her quirky sense of humor, MaryJanice Davidson launches what promises to be a smashing series with *Sleeping with the Fishes*. This book brought back the magic of first reading something new by this talented author. Her sense of humor and imagination know no bounds . . . pure delight to read from start to finish." —*A Romance Review*

"Davidson breathes new life into the frequently tired paranormal romance genre with this refreshingly witty entry featuring a decidedly bad-tempered half-mermaid named Fred . . . It will be interesting to see where Davidson goes with this new series." —*Monsters and Critics*

"Ms. Davidson is royalty in the ranks of paranormal comedy writers. Somehow, she manages to keep up a rapid-fire round of jokes without ever being too silly or skimping on characterization. It will be a fun trip to see how Fred's life develops in coming novels." —*The Eternal Night*

"An amusing and sexy new series with a decidedly underwater twist. Employing her patented brand of offbeat humor and lighthearted fun, she serves up a new heroine whose life is about to get extremely complicated." —*Romantic Times*

continued . . .

"You will spend many an hour just laughing through her books."*

**Praise for
the Undead novels of MaryJanice Davidson**

"Delightful, wicked fun!" —Christine Feehan

"A lighthearted vampire pastiche that recalls the work of Charlaine Harris." —*Omaha World-Herald*

"Chick lit meets vampire action in this creative, sophisticated, sexy, and wonderfully witty book." —Catherine Spangler

"A laugh-a-minute book." —**Romance Junkies*

"Davidson delivers more wildly witty, irreverent, and just plain funny adventures in her patently hilarious style." —*Romantic Times* (4½ stars)

"One of the funniest, most satisfying series to come along lately. If you're [a] fan of Sookie Stackhouse and Anita Blake, don't miss Betsy Taylor. She rocks." —*The Best Reviews*

"I don't care what mood you are in, if you open this book you are practically guaranteed to laugh . . . top-notch humor and a fascinating perspective of the vampire world." —*ParaNormal Romance Reviews*

"[A] wickedly clever and amusing romp. Davidson's witty dialogue, fast pacing, smart plotting, laugh-out-loud humor, and sexy relationships make this a joy to read." —*Booklist*

Swimming Without a Net

MaryJanice Davidson

JOVE BOOKS, NEW YORK

THE BERKLEY PUBLISHING GROUP
Published by the Penguin Group
Penguin Group (USA) Inc.
375 Hudson Street, New York, New York 10014, USA
Penguin Group (Canada), 90 Eglinton Avenue East, Suite 700, Toronto, Ontario M4P 2Y3, Canada
(a division of Pearson Penguin Canada Inc.)
Penguin Books Ltd., 80 Strand, London WC2R 0RL, England
Penguin Group Ireland, 25 St. Stephen's Green, Dublin 2, Ireland (a division of Penguin Books Ltd.)
Penguin Group (Australia), 250 Camberwell Road, Camberwell, Victoria 3124, Australia
(a division of Pearson Australia Group Pty. Ltd.)
Penguin Books India Pvt. Ltd., 11 Community Centre, Panchsheel Park, New Delhi—110 017, India
Penguin Group (NZ), 67 Apollo Drive, Rosedale, North Shore 0632, New Zealand
(a division of Pearson New Zealand Ltd.)
Penguin Books (South Africa) (Pty.) Ltd., 24 Sturdee Avenue, Rosebank, Johannesburg 2196,
South Africa

Penguin Books Ltd., Registered Offices: 80 Strand, London WC2R 0RL, England

This is a work of fiction. Names, characters, places, and incidents either are the product of the author's imagination or are used fictitiously, and any resemblance to actual persons, living or dead, business establishments, events, or locales is entirely coincidental. The publisher does not have any control over and does not assume any responsibility for author or third party websites or their content.

SWIMMING WITHOUT A NET

A Jove Book / published by arrangement with the author

PRINTING HISTORY
Jove mass-market edition / December 2007

Copyright © 2007 by MaryJanice Alongi.
Excerpt from "Undead and Wed" by MaryJanice Davidson copyright © 2007
by MaryJanice Alongi.
Cover illustration by Brendan Dorman.
Cover design by Judith Lagerman.
Interior text design by Kristin del Rosario.

All rights reserved.
No part of this book may be reproduced, scanned, or distributed in any printed or electronic form without permission. Please do not participate in or encourage piracy of copyrighted materials in violation of the author's rights. Purchase only authorized editions.
For information, address: The Berkley Publishing Group,
a division of Penguin Group (USA) Inc.,
375 Hudson Street, New York, New York 10014.

ISBN: 978-0-515-14381-2

JOVE®
Jove Books are published by The Berkley Publishing Group,
a division of Penguin Group (USA) Inc.,
375 Hudson Street, New York, New York 10014.
JOVE is a registered trademark of Penguin Group (USA) Inc.
The "J" design is a trademark belonging to Penguin Group (USA) Inc.

PRINTED IN THE UNITED STATES OF AMERICA

10 9 8 7 6 5 4 3 2 1

If you purchased this book without a cover, you should be aware that this book is stolen property. It was reported as "unsold and destroyed" to the publisher, and neither the author nor the publisher has received any payment for this "stripped book."

This book is for everyone who was ever irritated by a Disney heroine. Detox with Fred, and rejoice!

It's also for my dear friend Cathie Carr, who had a crummy year, was lied to (repeatedly) by loved ones, deceived by friends (who had good intentions, but still), did everything she could to save her marriage only to be rewarded with a boot in the face (repeatedly), and managed to pick up the pieces anyway. I'm thirty-eight now, and I never thought I'd meet someone with a bigger pair of plums than mine. Cathie's plums make mine look like raisins. Or is that an overshare?

Acknowledgments

I could never write a book without adding an acknowledgments page (or two, or six). Some readers find this puzzling (and often annoying, but hey, nobody's sticking a gun to your head, right?), but for me it's always been simple.

All writers know they didn't create the book/story/play/commercial jingle/tampon ad on their own. Just having a partner to keep the kids out of your hair is worth a mention on the acknowledgments page. And I've been lucky enough to have far more than that.

My friends are quite jaded by now; when I told my buddy Todd he was getting a mention on the acknowledgments page, he said, "Can't you send me cash instead?" Yeah, well, drop dead twice, O'Halloran.

So! Thanks, in no particular order, are due to: my husband and coauthor (we write the Jennifer Scales series together), my children, my sister, my parents. My agent, my editor, the copy editors, the line editors. The marketing reps, the catalog designers, the cover designers, the flap copy writers.

See, I just put a bunch of gibberish out and it happens to land on a page. The people mentioned above are the ones who take a messy, 300-plus page rough draft and turn it into a book. Maybe even a great book.

For this book in particular, I ended the first draft on page 200. Even for me, notorious for my tight (read: short) single titles, 200 pages is BAD. Even 300 is skating on the edge. As I explained to my editor, "I got nothin'." I got to the end, it was done, the story was told, and I was on page 200.

So Cindy, bless her heart, read the manuscript and sent me a page of suggestions. Pointed out where I broke Awful Writing Rule #1: I told, not showed. Suggested scenes I skipped altogether (it's because of Cindy that we saw Moon Bimm again, and speculation about Fred's mysterious merman father started up so quickly). Because of Cindy, we saw Dr. Barb in the Caymans and the disaster (and Jonas pummeling) that nearly followed.

(Also, for those of you who haven't read the preceding book, *Sleeping with the Fishes*, fear not: I think I did a pretty good job explaining the events in that book. You shouldn't be too lost. But hey, if you are, just buy the first book!)

(Go ahead. We'll wait.)

(We're still waiting, here. You think we've got nothing better to—)

(Ah. Very good. Thanks. Great cover, huh?)

I must warn you, dear readers, that there is an act of somewhat annoying violence in this book, an act I pretty much glossed over. Cindy coaxed a truer scene out of me, one more suited to the situation and the story and the characters.

The end result, I think, was not only a longer book (my true goal) but, thanks to Cindy Hwang, a better book.

The latter, of course, is up to you, dear reader. And so, finally, thanks for picking up the book and giving it a try. If the cover caught your eye, hooray! If it was the flap copy, even better. If it was name recognition, that's swell. But as every reader knows, there are all kinds of reasons to pluck a book off the shelf . . . or not.

So thanks for the pluck. I'll try not to let you down.

MaryJanice Davidson
www.maryjanicedavidson.net

Author's Note

Note from the author (that's me!): The actions of Fred's third blind date were inspired by the fabulous movie *Better Off Dead*, starring John Cusack. I must have watched that movie a thousand times as a teenager. I saw a chance to pay homage to one of my all-time favorites, and jumped at it.

Swimming
Without
a Net

Not everything is a mermaid that dives into the water.

—RUSSIAN PROVERB

I declare that civil war is inevitable and is near at hand.

—SAM HOUSTON, AMERICAN GENERAL

I started early, took my dog,
And visited the sea;
The mermaids in the basement
Came out to look at me.
And frigates in the upper floor
Extended hempen hands,
Presuming me to be a mouse,
Aground, upon the sands.

—EMILY DICKINSON, Part II, Nature

To Jove, and all the other Deities,
Thou must exhibit solemn sacrifice;
And then the black sea for thee shall be clear.

—*The Odysseys of Homer*

The greatest trick the devil ever pulled was convincing the world he didn't exist.

—BAUDELAIRE, *Le Joueur généreux*

One

Fredrika Bimm trudged down Comm Ave. (known to tourists and other mysterious creatures as Commonwealth Avenue, Boston, Massachusetts) and tried not to think about the Prince of the Black Sea, or famed romance novelist Priscilla D'Jacqueline.

She had, in fact, spent the better part of the last twelve months determinedly *not* thinking about them.

And why should she? She had a fulfilling job. Okay, an irritating job. She had her own home, which she never had to herself anymore. She had a best friend who was infatuated with a new girlfriend and never had time for her anymore.

A pity party already. And not even two o'clock! A new record!

It was a typically lovely autumn afternoon—yawn— and her Wordsworth book bag bulged with D'Jacqueline's last two novels, *Passion's Searing Flames* and *The Rake and the Raconteur*. This did not count as thinking about Thomas Pearson, a fellow marine biologist who made big bucks writing under the D'Jacqueline pen name. This was supporting a colleague. That was all.

A colleague with brown hair and lush red highlights, broad shoulders, long legs, and dimples. A colleague who carried a switchblade among other various illegal weapons. A colleague who told her he loved her and then left for eleven months and fourteen days.

"Stop it!" she yowled aloud, ignoring the startled looks of passersby. "He had his fellowship to finish and he only knew you a week so just cut it out! What are *you* looking at?" she added fiercely, and the kindergarten-age child scuttled behind her mother's legs.

No, Thomas was gone and that was all. So was Artur,

for that matter, the *other* man she determinedly did not think about. A full-blooded member of the Undersea Folk—a merman, in other words. Not a half-and-half hybrid like herself.

More than that: a prince, the eldest son of the High King of the Black Sea. A prince with hair the color of rubies and eyes the color of cherry cough drops; a prince with big hands he couldn't keep to himself. And a red beard that tickled whenever he *did things she would not think about.*

She stopped at her brownstone, practically ran up the stairs, jammed her key in the lock, and rushed into the foyer. Too keyed up for the elevator, she walked the three flights to her apartment and almost knocked the door down instead of fumbling with her key.

She kicked the door shut behind her and snarled, "What are you two doing here?"

"Waiting for you," her best friend, Jonas Carrey, chirped. He was a tall blond, a couple of inches taller than she, who held several black belts and loved appletinis. Oh, and her boss, Dr. Barb, who was currently sitting on his lap.

"Dr. Barb," Fred sighed, tossing her book bag onto the nearest counter.

"Dr. Bimm." Her boss was a stickler for titles under all circumstances, even if Jonas's hand was trying to undo her bra clasp.

"Dr. Barb, you've been dating my friend for a year. Don't you think it's time you called me Fred?"

"No, Dr. Bimm."

Fred sighed again. She liked her boss, under normal circumstances, but since the woman had started banging her best friend, it was harder and harder to be around the two of them.

For one thing, they were still in the "oooh goo oooh" stage of courtship, when anything either of them did was greeted with cries of delight. Jonas could find a worm in his oatmeal and Dr. Barb would find it charming.

For another thing, like most couples, they felt all Fred's problems would be solved if only she could Find Someone. To that end . . .

"Sam's going to be here any minute," Jonas informed her, like she could forget. "Is that, um, what you're wearing?"

4

"Yes." She almost snapped. For the hundredth time, she wished she hadn't given Jonas a set of her keys. She never knew when she'd find him (them) lurking in her apartment. "Why, what's the matter?"

"Besides the fact that it's sixty degrees out and you're wearing cutoffs and a T-shirt? And would it kill you to wear a bra?"

Fred barely restrained a sniff. As a mermaid, she didn't much notice the cold—Jonas ought to try the Arctic sometime if he thought Massachusetts autumns were chilly. And, frankly, she didn't need a bra. Never had. Either gravity was being kind, or it was another benefit of her half-and-half heritage.

"At least a pedicure," Jonas was begging. "And brush your hair. You'd be so gorgeous if you—"

"That's not nice," Dr. Barb said reproachfully. Jonas had performed one of his miraculous makeovers on her just before they'd started going out, and it had gone straight to his head.

Normally tightly bound in a braid, Dr. Barb's beautiful dark blond hair now tumbled halfway down her back. Her almond-shaped eyes were carefully made-up,

5

and she was wearing a tailored red suit. Her tiny, red pump–shod feet dangled several inches above the floor and she snuggled farther into Jonas's lap.

"Fred doesn't need any help to look good," her besotted boss was saying. Fred, meanwhile, had opened her fridge and was desperately hunting for a beer. Or Drano. "You leave her be."

"Sorry, baby."

"You're forgiven, for a kiss."

"Two kisses!"

Fred kept hunting. Could she get drunk off of two measly wine coolers? Maybe if she spiked them with the spoiled milk . . .

"Done!" Jonas cried, and then various smacking noises cut off the annoying conversation. Of course, now she was dealing with a whole new set of annoying, but—

"Success!" She snatched the Miller Lite left over from some party. Let's see, the last party Jonas had made her host had been in the twentieth century . . . Did beer go bad? Oh, who cared?

"Your hair is so soft," Dr. Barb sighed, running her fingers through Jonas's carefully coiffed locks.

"So is yours, baby, but you should use more of that deep conditioner I left at your place." Jonas was a chemical scientist who worked for Aveda, and was always dropping off free product. Fred ignored it, but Dr. Barb took it to heart. "Just wrap your hair in a towel and leave it in for half an hour or so, then rinse."

"I will . . ." Fred looked around for a bottle opener, then gave up and wrenched the cap off with her bare hand. "For a kiss."

Fred guzzled.

"Done!" More smacking sounds.

Fred finished the beer and noted, with despair, that her damned superior metabolism had taken care of any meager alcohol offered by the good people at Miller, Inc. She should have known. But desperate times called for desperate—

"I love your eyes," Dr. Barb sighed, coming up for air.

"I love yours," Jonas said, caressing Barb's long strands of hair.

"I could look into yours all day and never get tired of the view," Dr. Barb said, stroking Jonas's shoulder.

Jonas nibbled on her ear in response. Fred coldly watched the primates groom each other and actually wished her blind date—the third in two weeks—would show up already.

In answer to her prayer, there was a sharp rap at her door.

"Oh thank God," she mumbled. Then, louder, "Get out, you two. I've got to go. Uh . . . what's this one's name again?"

"Sam Fisher," Dr. Barb said patiently.

Fred shot Jonas a look. Dr. Barb didn't know Fred was a mermaid . . . yet. "Is that supposed to be a joke?"

"We had the same advisor in graduate school. It's not his fault he ended up in marine biology."

"Out!"

"We're going, we're going," Jonas said.

"I'm sure you'll just love him," Dr. Barb said doubtfully, climbing out of Jonas's lap. "You'll have lots to talk about."

"And brush your hair before you take off," Jonas added, following his ladylove to the door. Jonas yanked it open, nearly got a fist in the face (Sam liked to knock, lots, and *loud*), and said, "Nice to meet you, good-bye."

The door shut behind them and Fred sized up her latest blind date.

To her amusement, he was frowning at her. Tall and whip thin, with wire-rimmed glasses and a shaved head, he had the most amazing green eyes she'd ever seen, the color of moss on a rainy day.

"Hi," she said. "I'm Fred Bimm."

"Sam Fisher. Look, the only reason I'm here is because Barb has been on my ass to hook up ever since she started getting laid regularly."

Fred swallowed a cough of surprise. "It's, ah, nice to meet you, too."

He raised an eyebrow at her. "And I bet *you're* only here—besides the fact that you live here—because *your* friend wants you to hook up, too."

"It's not the only reason."

He frowned at her.

"It's the only reason," she admitted.

"I'm perfectly happy with my life right now, not to mention you're too young for me."

"I'm thirty," she protested.

"A mere infant. Also, my TiVo is on the fritz and if I take you to dinner, I'm going to miss *Lost*."

"You're trying to get out of a date to watch TV?"

"It's the season opener!"

Fred shrugged. "They're not going to really tell you anything. You know that, right? Every week is just another hand-job, courtesy of ABC."

Sam's frown deepened. "If the subtle clues fly over your head, that's not ABC's fault."

"Hey!"

"But as I was saying. Assuming we went on this travesty of a date—"

"Hey!" Fred was used to being the most irritating person in the room. Sam's attitude was startling, to put it mildly.

"—we'd take the T to Le Meridien—I'd treat for the subway tokens."

"I have a T card," Fred volunteered.

"Fine. We'd have drinks and dinner and, since I'm a generous tipper . . ." He tipped his head back and stared at the ceiling. "Call it a hundred fifty bucks."

"No dessert?"

He ignored her. "Then we might decide to take in a late show. Call it another twenty bucks. Plus popcorn and drinks. Another twenty-five."

"I'd still be full from dinner. No popcorn for me."

"Nothing must be left to chance. So that brings us to

10

one hundred ninety-five dollars. But since you're a modern woman, you'll insist on paying for half."

"Also, I don't want to feel obligated to put out."

"Too right. Which makes your share ninety-seven dollars and fifty cents."

Sam waited expectantly. Fred swallowed a grin and said, "Will you take a check?"

Two

🐚

"So that's what you do? All day? You feed fish?"
Blind Date Number Four (she could not remember the
man's name for her life) asked, forking more linguine
with clams into his maw, which was always open—
either for food or inane chatter.

"That's all," Fred replied, repressing a shudder and at-
tacking her salad like a moray eel going after an angelfish.
She was allergic to shellfish and watching Number Four
shovel it in was fairly nauseating. "I feed the fish, make
sure the little ones aren't getting chomped, like that."

12

"I think I've see you in the tank!" Number Four ex-claimed, and a tiny piece of masticated clam hit Fred's left cheek. "You're one of the guys in the scuba suits who hang out in that big tank."

"Main One," she corrected him, concealing a shud-der as she wiped her cheek with a napkin. It was telling how much this one was irritating her; she never called it Main One. That was strictly a Dr. Barb rule. "And I doubt you've seen me."

If he'd seen her flailing around in her wet suit, he cer-tainly would have remembered. She couldn't swim with legs; only with her tail. It made her job trickier than it had to be, for sure. For one thing, she always ended up upside down in Main One, and her scuba gear always tried its best to get tangled, despite her years of certification.

"I monitor the water levels and pull out any sick fish and stuff like that."

"Cool! So what's that pay?"

She gave him an odd look. Number Four had man-aged to work money into the conversation a record seven times. She already knew what his house cost, what his annual salary was, what his tax bite was, and what a flight to Tokyo cost these days.

"Enough to keep a roof over my head."

"I'm gonna say fifty," he guessed. He looked like an accountant—brown suit, brown hair, mud-colored eyes, stubby fingers. Not unattractive, just . . . blah. "Fifty K. You've got an advanced degree, that's gotta be worth some bucks."

Fred laughed. "Shows what you know about advanced degrees . . . and private nonprofits."

"So quit and work in the public sector."

"I like my job."

"I bet you could make six figures in the public sector."

"Sure, thinking up new and improved crap to dump in the ocean. No thanks."

"Six figures!" Number Four repeated, spraying more clam sauce.

"Don't care. Don't need it. Getting bored."

"Want dessert?"

"Hell, no."

For the third time, Fred explained to Number Four that he didn't need to drive her to her apartment in his new Lexus hybrid ($75,000, after rebate).

"It's just twenty minutes by subway. I'll be fine."

"Oh, come on. Leather seats!"

"I'm all atingle," she replied. They were walking past the restaurant toward the Park Street T stop. "Really."

"Then how about something for my trouble?"

"Nope."

"Leather seats!"

"Go away," she told Number Four.

"Aw, come on! I took the whole afternoon off for you."

It was true; it hadn't been dinner, it had been lunch. Dr. Barb had given her the day off, which should have instantly roused her suspicions.

"And I'm pathetically grateful. Good night."

He reached out and seized her arm. "Just one kiss," he said, breathing clams and garlic in her face. "And maybe a hand-job."

Fred blinked. It wasn't that she was inexperienced, or a prude. She just hadn't met an asshole of this magnitude since she, Thomas, and Artur had killed Dr. Barb's ex-husband last fall.

She smiled at him. She wished, in that moment, she'd inherited the sharp teeth of her father's people instead of

15

the flat grinders of Homo sapiens. "I'll be happy to give you a hand-job," she said.

"Great!" He yanked her by the elbow toward the cemetery outside the T stop. "C'mere, we can have some privacy."

"No need for that," she said, effortlessly extricating herself from his grip, seizing each of his thumbs, and popping them out of their sockets.

He didn't scream so much as whinny, and bent forward to cradle his odd-looking thumbs between his thighs.

"Thanks for dinner," she said, stepping around him and already fishing for her T card.

Three

🦄

Fred saw the lights on in her apartment and stomped up the stairs. This time she'd give Jonas a piece of her mind, as well as Dr. Barb, never mind that the woman was her boss. Enough was enough! Clam globs in her face, garlic breath, sexual harassment. And it wasn't even Wednesday!

She unlocked her door and shoved it open, and was momentarily startled to see the happy couple sitting stiffly on her couch as opposed to grooming each other or, worse, getting to third base.

Standing just inside her doorway were two strangers. One was a young man—early twenties?—with startling orange hair (jack-o'-lantern orange) and matching eyes. Beside him was a petite young woman of about the same age, with dark blue hair and eyes that were even darker, the way small sapphires almost looked black in the right light.

She knew at once they were Undersea Folk, and mentally she groaned. Apparently the high point of her day was going to be dislocating Number Four's thumbs.

Before either stranger could speak, Jonas leapt up from the couch, said (too heartily), "Good, great, you're here, we told your friends we'd wait with them, but now you're here so we'll be going, see you, good-bye."

"Good-bye," Dr. Barb managed as Jonas dragged her out the door. "Young lady, whoever does your hair is doing a magnificent—"

Jonas slammed the door.

Fred surveyed the mermaid and merman. "Hit me," she said at last.

The two exchanged puzzled glances. "Those are not our instructions," the man said. "I am Kertal. This is Tennian. We were sent by the High King."

"Well, I didn't think you were here to take a survey. Something to drink? Some chips?"

"No, thank you," the woman—Tennian—said in a soft, lovely alto. "You are Fredrika Bimm, of Kortrim's line."

"If Kortrim is my bio-dad, you're right. But I prefer to think of myself as being of Moon Bimm's line. That's my mother," she added helpfully.

"Yes, His Highness has told us of your lady mother," Kertal said. He towered over her and had the ropy muscles of a long-distance swimmer. Which, of course, he was. She was having a terrible time not staring at him. Both of them. Their coloring was so extraordinary! It was odd to be in a room and not feel like she had the freakiest hair there. "We were instructed to try you at your home if we did not find you at the aquarium."

"You went to where I *work*?"

"Yes."

"Oh my God," Fred said, and collapsed on her couch.

"We asked of you, and spoke of you to your friends. They brought us to your"—Kertal looked around the tiny apartment with an unreadable expression on his face—"home."

"You didn't tell them who you were, did you?"

"Our business is with you, not them."

"I'm going to take that as a no." She rolled over and stared at the ceiling. "Thank God. My boss doesn't know I'm a mermaid and I'd like to keep it that way."

Again, the two strangers exchanged glances, and again, it was Kertal who spoke. "We are charged by the High King to summon you to the Pelagic."

"The Pelagic?" Fred could almost feel her mind buckle under the strain and she giggled until she lost her breath. "I don't know what you guys think it is, but here a pelagic is an open zone in the ocean that's not near a coast or even a sea floor. How can you bring me to *a* pelagic? And will you sit down? You look like a couple of Army recruiters. Unclench."

Neither of them moved. "A Pelagic is a meeting that can only be called by a majority of the Undersea Folk."

"I thought you guys were a monarchy."

"Our good king has acceded to the request of his people," Tennian almost whispered.

"Can you speak up, please? It's hard to hear you over the roaring in my ears."

"Will you come?" Tennian asked, slightly louder.

"To this Pelagic thing? Sorry, I'll need a little more info before I go gallivanting off with you two. Like, what exactly is it? Where is it? And why am I invited? And will you two *sit down*? I'm freaked out enough."

The two Undersea Folk gingerly sat on her kitchen chairs. Fred's apartment was an open design. The kitchen, the dining room, and the living room were all one big space. The small bedroom was off to the left, the bathroom off to the right.

Fred had fooled the eye into thinking the place was large and airy by painting all the walls white. The place was stark enough to belong to a monk, which suited her fine. She hated clutter.

She spotted the brand-new Aveda bag beside the kitchen chair, and nudged it beneath the table with a toe. "So. You were saying?"

"As you know, Fredrika, the royal family makes its home in the Black Sea. It is also the seat of our government."

"Right, the king and Artur. Got it."

"And His Highness Rankon, and Her Highness Jeredna."

"He's got sibs? He never said. And would it kill you guys to have a Jenny or a Peter?"

"It is not for us to know the workings of the royal mind," Tennian murmured.

"Ha! I know all about the workings of Artur's mind, and he's only got one thing on it. That's— Never mind. You were saying?"

"May I have a glass of water?" Kertal asked.

"Sure." Fred jumped up, glad to have something to do. She guessed what Kertal's problem was—simple dehydration—and filled two glasses, one for each of them, to the top. As Artur had told her last year, Undersea Folk could walk around on land, but not for long, and they weakened quickly.

Tiny Tennian drained hers in three gulps and politely asked for a refill. And another. Thus, it was a good five minutes before either of them got back to the subject at hand.

"I assume you guys hang out in the Black Sea because it's enclosed? Easier to stay hidden? I mean, up here, you're—we're—myths. No one's been able to prove the Undersea Folk exist."

"You are correct, Fredrika," Kertal said, setting his

empty glass down on the kitchen table. "Your studies of the sea have served you well."

"Yes, I have my name on all sorts of pretty papers."

"Many centuries ago the royal family chose the Black Sea for precisely that reason. That is not to say we all live there; the Undersea Folk are scattered all over the world."

"I live in Chesapeake Bay," Tennian whispered.

"But the seat of power has always been in the Black Sea. However, there are so many of us, and it can be a difficult place to get to in a short time without rousing suspicion. So the Pelagic will be held in the waters of the Cayman Islands."

"Ah, the glorious Caymans. What are you, repping the chamber of commerce?"

"No," Kertal the Humorless replied. "We will wait while you collect your things."

"Hold up, hold up. So this Pelagic, the purpose of which neither of you have bothered to explain, won't be where the royal family hangs out, and we won't be going to Turkey. But we'll have a fine time hanging out in the Caymans."

"I do not know how fine a time it will be," Kertal said soberly.

"Oh, here we go."

"Many of our people do not wish to remain myths."

"Oh, ho."

"This goes directly against the wishes of the royal family."

"Fascinating."

"Thus, the Pelagic: a meeting of all Folk, to decide a common action. They are quite rare; the last one was held—ah—" He glanced at Tennian and the small woman shook her head. "—was a while ago. Decades."

Fred smelled a rat. Or a fish. But there was time to get to the bottom of that later. "So you guys are getting together to figure out whether to go public or not?"

"Not 'you guys.' All of us. You, too, Fredrika."

She raised an eyebrow. "Is that a fact?"

"The High King insists."

"So? I'm not one of his subjects."

"Excuse me," Tennian murmured, "but you are."

"Want to arm wrestle for it?"

"The king requires your presence," Kertal droned on. "As does His Highness, Prince Artur."

"And I'm *definitely* not at *his* beck and call. Sorry you

came all this way for nothing, help yourselves to more water, good-bye."

"The prince suspected you would be . . . intractable."

She folded her arms across her chest. "Try unbudgeable."

"He asked us to remind you that he saved your life."

"He didn't stop me from getting shot!" And why was the thought of seeing the redheaded bum again so thrilling? Not to mention the idea of meeting other Undersea Folk. Of course, if they were all as stodgy as these two, it'd be a long time in the Caymans. Which reminded her . . . "How long is this Pelagic supposed to last?"

"Until the majority comes to an agreement, approved by His Majesty."

"But that could take—I have no idea how long that could take. How many mer-dudes will show up?"

"Thousands."

"*Thousands?*"

"Perhaps. There is no way to tell."

"Is there anything you *can* commit to?"

"We cannot leave without your agreement and attendance."

"Oh, friggin' swell." Fred rested her chin on her fist and thought. The other two watched her do it, and said nothing. Finally she said, "Is Artur sending duos of ambassadors to *all* the Undersea Folk?"

Again, they exchanged a look. But this time Tennian spoke up. Barely. "No. You are considered a special case, and essential to this gathering."

"According to whom?"

"The entire royal family."

Fred gave thanks she was sitting down, because otherwise she was fairly certain she would have fallen on her ass.

Four

"But why?" she managed after gasping like a landed trout.

"It is not for us to know."

"Just 'go fetch Fred,' is that it?"

"Yes," Kertal replied.

"And I'm supposed to pack a bag and follow you guys to the Caymans?"

"Yes."

"And if I don't?"

"You owe a debt to the royal family," Kertal reminded her.

"And you're a subject," Tennian added unhelpfully.

"I am not! And I do not." Still. Talk about a once in a lifetime opportunity. The marine biologist in her was itching to get a look at a meeting populated with thousands of mermaids. But it chafed, being ordered to go like that. Shit, her mom had quit trying to give her orders by the fourth grade.

She wondered how the other Folk knew to come to the Caymans, then remembered how her father's people communicated: by telepathy. Duh. How *else* did you talk underwater?

Fred opened her mouth to argue more when she heard the rattle of keys and her front door burst open. Jonas was framed in the doorway, panting, clutching her doorknob so hard his knuckles were white. "What'd I miss?"

"Apparently I'm going to the Caymans."

"How come?"

"Super secret mermaid business."

Her friend beamed. "Great! I'll go pack your things. Good thing you've got tons of vacation time coming. Don't worry, I'll fix it with Barb."

Fred covered her face with her hands. "Shit."

"Will I need a passport?"

"You're not coming," she tried, already knowing the outcome.

"Ha! Think I'll miss out on a chance to stock up on some of that yummy rum? And do you know how long it's been since I've had a vacation? Never mind how long it's been since *you've* had one." To Tennian and Kertal: "Classic workaholic, you guys. No hope at all." To Fred: "Besides, you'll just get into trouble by yourself."

"Sir, you are not invited," Kertal said.

"Sir, I'd like to see you stop me. I would also like to find out who does your hair."

"Bipeds are not welcome," Tennian mumbled.

"And *your* hair."

Fred saw her chance, and jumped at it. "I'm only going if he goes." Had she really just said that? She mentally replayed the last five seconds. Yes, she had. "That's the deal. Take it or leave it."

This time, the Grim Duo didn't bother exchanging glances. They just nodded in perfect weird unison.

"Woo-hoo!" Jonas yowled. "I'll go pack my swim trunks."

Five

🦐

"I don't know why you're so excited," Fred grumbled as Jonas stomped on the accelerator. As it was fall, and midweek, traffic to Cape Cod was light. And Jonas was enjoying his new toy, a gray Ford hybrid. "I haven't even decided to go."

"Yuh-huh!" He beeped the horn at a dawdling tourist—they both hated it when morons went fifty miles an hour in the passing zone—and whipped past the small blue Volkswagen.

Fred slammed her finger down on the window button

and yowled into the wind, "Passing zone is for passing, shithead!"

"Don't make me put the child locks on the windows again," Jonas warned. "And you did so say you were going. You told what's-their-names you'd go if I could go."

"Yeah, well, I lost my temper there for a second. Frankly, I can't figure out why we're even going to my mom's."

"Because *nice* and *loving* daughters *tell* their hot moms when they're *leaving* the *country*."

"That's enough about my hot mom," Fred warned, knowing it was no use. The former hippie, Moon Bimm, was in ridiculously good shape for a woman in her early fifties. To Fred's eternal despair, she had personal knowledge that Moon still had the sex drive of an eighteen-year-old.

"Say," Jonas said cheerfully, reading her mind as usual, "remember last year when you walked in on her and Sam doing the wild thing on the—"

Fred jabbed the volume button.

"Didn't your stepfather have to go see a chiropractor after you threw him off your mom?" Jonas screamed over the music.

Fred rolled the window back down and stuck her head out, doglike, for the next half hour.

"Come on, show me," Jonas begged.

So she took her friend around the side of the cream-colored Cape Cod house with the hunter green shutters, and showed him the now-fixed sliding glass kitchen door. The one she'd broken through last fall when she thought her mother was in danger at the hands of a merman. The first one she'd ever met.

"Jeez," Jonas said, impressed. He rapped his knuckles on the glass. "This shit is *thick*. And you just walked through it?"

"Kicked it in. Then walked."

"The extreme always makes an impression," Jonas said, quoting a line from his all-time favorite movie, *Heathers*. He'd had an absurd crush on Winona Ryder since *Mermaids*.

"Then what?"

"Then I met Artur, High Prince of the Undersea Folk, whom I had assumed was committing felony assault on my folks."

"Not knowing," Jonas added, having begged to hear

the story about a thousand times, "that Moon had already charmed him with her extreme hotness and everything was fine."

"Anyway," she continued with a glare, "Sam got the door fixed the next day, end of story."

"Ah, Sam. Ridiculously fortunate (wealthy) hubby to the delicious Moon, trodden stepfather to the grumpiest mermaid on the planet. Agh!"

Fred flinched, then looked. The man in question, her stepfather, was blinking at them through the glass (and his bifocals). Sam was a few inches shorter than Fred, with graying brown hair pulled back in his usual ponytail, which only highlighted his bald spot.

He hit the latch and slid the door open. "Hello, Fred. Jonas. We have a guest." Code for: ix-nay on the ermaid-may uff-stay.

"We won't stay long," Fred promised, stepping past her stepfather.

"Maybe only for dessert. Did Moon make ice cream again?" Jonas asked.

"Are you kidding?" Sam smiled and opened the freezer. "What's your favorite flavor?"

"Wh-who's that?" a trembling voice asked.

Sam stretched out one of his rough amateur carpenter's hands and, after a long moment, a little girl (Fred put her age at about five, unless she was malnourished, which was certainly likely given her bone structure and large, almost bulging brown eyes) reached out and grasped one of Sam's fingers. "Ellie, this is my daughter, Fred, and her best friend, Jonas."

Ellie was now standing almost behind Sam, and Fred could only see one big brown eye. Jonas, busily building himself a six-scoop sundae, looked up from licking a spoon and waved.

"Who's he?" Ellie whispered.

Sam knelt, very slowly, and took Ellie by the shoulders, very gently. "That is my daughter's very best friend in the world. He was picked on all the time in school and Fred had to watch out for him. She protected him. He would never, ever hurt you."

"But you don't know." Ellie's expression had the faraway look of a child in a nightmare she would never wake from. "Only God knows everything."

Fred coughed, which caused Sam and Ellie to look over at her. "Hey, Ellie. Watch this."

Mentally apologizing to her oldest friend, Fred seized Jonas by the shirt collar and heaved him out of his chair and through the (fortunately open) sliding door.

Six

Jonas was densely built ("Deliciously so." Dr. Barb might have said over the sound of Fred's retching), but no match for Fred's hybrid strength, and the air velocity he achieved was really quite something.

Fred ignored his wail ("My sundaeeee!"), which became easier to do the fainter it got. "See that, Ellie? Like Sam said, my friend would never hurt you. But if he did, if he contracted rabies and went crazy and actually tried to put his hands on you in a way you didn't like, I'd kick his balls up so high, he'd choke on them. 'Kay?"

Ellie edged around Sam and peered up at Fred. "Do you work out?"

"No, I hate gyms. And I hate tracks. I never work out if I can help it. Well, I swim." She thought, something so fun and necessary wasn't really *working out*, was it? "A lot."

Fred, of course, had known about the foster children her mother and Sam had been taking in. Some only stayed a week or two while various paperwork plodded through the system. Some only stayed a few hours. And some, like Ellie, had been around for months, because Sam was the only adult male she would tolerate. Ellie had been known to set fires around males who frightened her. Burning to death, she had explained to an ER attending (as well as several social workers), was preferable to Being Touched Like That Again.

The girl, as terrifying as she was vulnerable, was looking up at her. "I like your hair," she almost whispered.

"Thanks." Fred self-consciously fingered her greenish strands. "Can Jonas come back in?"

"It's your house," Ellie pointed out, holding out her hands in a gesture of helplessness which showed Fred the severe scars crawling up and down the girl's forearms.

"Actually, it's Sam's house," Fred corrected her

mildly, gnawing on the inside of her lower lip so she wouldn't shake the biological father's address out of the kid. "And my mom's. But if you don't want him to come back in, he can have his ice cream on the lawn."

"I hate youuuuuu," Jonas's voice floated in.

To Fred's amazement, the solemn, damaged child smiled. "He can come in. As long as you're here."

"As you wish, Ellie." Sam knelt and gently pulled the little girl around until she was standing in front of him. "But even if Fred wasn't here, I would protect you. You know that, don't you?"

"Yes, Sam. I have to go. Commercial's over." She walked out of the kitchen without another word.

"What the hell?" Jonas bitched, walking back in while brushing leaves out of his not-so-perfectly coiffed hair. "Do you ever ask yourself why you don't have a large social circle, Fred? Do you?"

"Sorry." She wasn't. "Had to make a point for the foster kid du jour."

"Oh, right. I forgot. But jeez! A little warning next time! Thanks for aiming me at the big pile of leaves."

"Welcome," she said, pretending she had done so on purpose. "Finish your sundae, you slob."

"Hey, I'm crawling with leaves and dead bugs and I *still* look better than you do."

This was true, so Fred dismissed the argument and turned to Sam, seeing him with new eyes. Oh, he *looked* the same. Myopic brown peepers blinking almost constantly, slim build, small potbelly, the perpetual ponytail.

He'd been there from her earliest memory, and she'd always known he hadn't been her *real* father, even though her mother hadn't told her so until Fred was nearly thirty. For heaven's sake, Sam panicked in a tide pool, whereas Fred had been breaststroking alongside wild dolphins since she was seven.

No, Sam was Sam, and for once she was grateful, for she realized how much this gentle man had to offer a child, any child. Certainly he treated her mother like a queen. And not out of fear of what Fred would do to him, either.

In fact, she was forced to admit to herself, it couldn't be easy having a mermaid for a stepdaughter, especially one as, uh, passionate as she was.

"What kind of marks are on her arm?" she asked abruptly, because the last thing she was going to do was go all mushy on *Sam* of all people. "Kitchen knife?"

"You should see her back," Sam said quietly, taking off his glasses and wiping them furiously on his faded Rolling Stones T-shirt. "Box cutter. Her dad works in a liquor warehouse. Likes to keep one on him for emergencies."

"File."

He blinked at her with watery brown eyes and put the glasses back on. "Sorry?"

"Her file. Gimme."

Sam actually smiled. "I was hoping you'd drop by, Fred, and her file is in my office, in your drawer."

Your drawer. A Sam-ism for a large file cabinet in the west corner of his office. Three feet deep, four drawers high. Never locked. Meticulously organized. Every drawing, every clay pot, every useless ashtray, every book report, every term paper Fred had come up with, from kindergarten to her doctoral thesis, was in that file cabinet. Sam had always left notes, books for her to read, information he wanted her to have, in the top drawer in the file marked "Fredly Fire." That's where Ellie's file would be. No doubt along with a copy of *Seven Highly Effective Habits for Undersea Folk*.

Sam usually put up a bit more of a fuss when it came

to violence, or proposed violence, so Fred narrowed her eyes at him and asked, "Isn't this the part where you preach peace and love?"

"I'll leave that, in this case, to your mother. Who is watching cartoons in the living room with Ellie. I'll go get her."

"Hey, Sam."

He turned and arched his graying brows.

"Thanks." And not just for Ellie. But she wouldn't—well, couldn't—get into that now.

Her stepfather nodded and padded out of the kitchen.

"Foster parents get files?" Jonas asked, scraping his bowl. "You'll be able to track down Daddy-o? Maybe pitch him headfirst into an industrial dryer and push Spin? Don't even think about going without me."

"Of course I'm thinking about going without you. Given Ellie's phobia around grown men, it's not hard to figure out who the bad guy is. And as a matter of fact, they *don't* give very detailed files. You know the term hacker, of course."

"Enlighten me, o brilliant fish tail," Jonas said with a mouth full of strawberry ice cream. "Pretend I'm an ignorant slob just like you."

"The term was *created* for Sam." Fred was smirking in spite of herself. She'd figured *that* out on her own by age ten. "He could use a computer as a spyglass before anyone knew it was possible. And he doesn't take a kid into his house until he knows *everything*."

"Not very hippielike," Jonas said, trying (and failing) to sound disapproving.

"Everybody's got bad habits."

"Fred! Sweetie!" Her mother, Moon, a short, good-looking blonde with silver streaks and shoulder-length hair, hurried into the kitchen and squeezed Fred so hard she nearly gasped. She was dressed in a faded pink T-shirt (one that had been red when Fred was a fourth grader) and jeans that clung to her chubby thighs. "What earth-shaking revelation brings you back home this time?"

"Earth-shaking," Jonas said with a mouthful of chocolate. "Ha!"

"Oh!" Moon jumped, then beamed. "Jonas, sweetie, I didn't see you there."

"That's because Fred's all hulking 'n stuff in the doorway. Great ice cream."

"I was not *hulking*."

"Did you find the banana?"

Jonas nodded. "It's beside the blueberry sorbet."

"How do you stay so slim?" her mother wondered, eyeing the remnants of the heroic sundae Jonas had nearly demolished.

"Clean living," he replied with his mouth full.

"And that cute new girlfriend, I bet." Moon winked.

"That cute new girlfriend is my boss, and let's change the subject," Fred interrupted, because Jonas and Moon could banter for hours. "I gotta leave town for a while."

"Business trip?"

"Yes," Fred said at the exact moment Jonas said, "No." They glared at each other.

"Uh-oh," her mother said, blue eyes twinkling. "And to think, it's been so dull around here the last few months. Except when Ellie forgot to put the top on the blender," she added thoughtfully, "and pushed Puree."

"It's no big deal, Mom."

"It's a *huge* deal, Moon," Jonas said. "You look great, by the way."

"I would find that flattering yet creepy," her mother said with a smile, "if I didn't know about your girlfriend. And as for you, Fredrika Bimm." The smile vanished. "I

43

wouldn't stand a lie from you when you were three. What makes you think anything's changed?"

"It's a Pelagic."

"Nor will I stand for your marine biologist geek-speak, which you so often use to avoid a direct answer. You can't hide behind language, young lady, so out with it."

Fred cursed the rotten luck of having a smart mother. "It's a meeting, okay? A meeting of all the Undersea Folk. You know, the name they use for themselves."

"It'll be Mermaid Central," Jonas added, "and Fred's ringside."

"Really?" Moon pulled up a chair and sat, leaning her elbows on the table. She was thinking so hard, her laugh lines were going the wrong way. "They're having a meeting and they invited you?"

"Yeah."

"Boggles the mind," Jonas added, "don't it?"

The laugh lines reversed and Moon's face lit up. "But that's wonderful!"

"Why," Fred asked suspiciously, "is it wonderful?"

"It means they're accepting you as one of them! And—and—"

44

Fred let her mother grope for words, not having the heart to say that Jonas, too, had an invitation to the Pelagic and certainly was *not* accepted by them. One didn't ensure the other. And Tennian and Kertal had been creepily vague.

She didn't like it. At all. She was only going because they'd gotten stubborn about Jonas and she couldn't resist jerking their chains. It had nothing to do with the possibility of seeing Artur again.

Nothing.

At all.

Shit, the guy was probably married with a wife who'd already popped out a litter of guppies. No, she had enough on her plate without worrying about Artur and who he'd been banging and what he'd been up to. Like . . . like . . .

Thomas! Thomas, for instance. She wondered what Thomas would think of the Pelagic. Shit, that was a lie. She knew exactly what he'd think. He was a marine biologist; he'd be wild to go.

Firmly, she shoved Artur and Thomas out of her mind and focused on what her mother was saying.

"—maybe even see your father again!"

Fred's jaw sagged and she clutched the back of the empty chair so hard she heard it crack. Here was a nightmare she had never even considered.

"You'd better sit down," Jonas worried. "You look really white. Even for you."

"I'm not going to the Caymans for a fucking family reunion!" she yowled.

"Oh, this Pelagic thing is in the Cayman Islands? Lovely this time of the year." Moon frowned. "I think. It's not hurricane season, is it?"

"Mom, I don't even know if my father will be there."

"It's a big meeting? Important? Obviously someone tracked you down and presented an invitation. That's a lot of trouble for, say, a slumber party."

"Yeah," Fred said grudgingly.

"So it's obviously a very important thing, this Paregoric, if they're tracking everybody down for it."

"Pelagic. A paregoric makes you pass out. On second thought," Fred admitted, "that might be the right name after all."

"Then he might be there! In fact, he's *sure* to be there!"

"Wait, wait, wait." Jonas held up a strawberry-stained

hand like a traffic cop gone off his diet. "I thought Artur said your dad was dead. Remember, last fall? Just before Fred broke down the kitchen door?"

"He said he *thought* Fred's dad was dead. That he hadn't been seen for many years. But the ocean is a big place." To Fred's dismay, Moon had that "everything will work out" expression on her face. "He could be alive! Sure he could! And Fred could meet him."

"Mom, I wouldn't know my bio-dad if he swam up to me and hooked me in the gut. And he wouldn't know me."

"Then I'll describe him," she said, and the horror continued. "He was built like a swimmer—"

"Ha, ha."

"—with the broad shoulders, you know, and the narrow waist? Oh, the body on your father! It was too dark to see his hair color, and besides, his hair was wet, but I imagine it's a darker shade of yours."

"Mom, I'm going to break Jonas's ice cream bowl and eat the pieces if you don't stop."

"His eyes were the purest green I'd ever seen, even darker than yours, sweetie. He was . . ." She looked over her shoulder, satisfying herself that Ellie and Sam were engrossed in SpongeBob. "He was the most mesmerizing creature I'd ever met."

"Vomit, vomit, vomit."

"I hardly noticed when he was inside me because I was just so enthralled by his eyes, his hair, his shoulders . . . and then it was done—"

"Mesmerizing," Jonas noted, "but fast."

"—and then he rolled off me and dove back into the ocean and I watched for him until dawn, but he never came back. I watched for him at that spot every night for three months." Moon sighed and looked out the kitchen window. "But he never came back."

"You want me to track that shitheel down? Fuck that!"

"Fredrika," her mom warned.

"Mom, he banged you and then he forgot about you. If I *do* find him, I plan on kicking the fins out of him. Nobody treats my mother like that!"

"Fredrika, Sam and I will not be here forever."

"Not the 'you gotta find a man' speech again, for crying out loud."

"I'm not implying you need a man to be happy. I'm saying your blood relatives are rare and wonderful

48

things. Yours in particular," she added, unconsciously eyeing Fred's hair. "If you could find your biological father . . . Even if it's true, even if he's dead, maybe you have . . . I don't know . . . aunts? Cousins?"

"Forget it, Mom. It's a Pelagic, not a family reunion." Whatever that meant. "I'm going to this meeting and that's it. Jonas thought we ought to stop by and let you know we'll be out of town for a while." And it was for just this sort of reason that she tended to avoid trips to the Cape. "Oh, and I gotta get something out of Sam's office. And then we're out of here."

"Will Prince Artur be there?"

Fred groaned. "Yes."

"It's a regular Hottie Convention," Jonas said. "It's just stupid how all the Undersea Folk are gorgeous."

"Hmmm," her mother said.

"What, 'hmmm'?"

"It's amazing how a person such as myself, generally open and friendly, could have raised such a suspicious creature."

"Well, so what if you did?" Fred snapped. "Who cares if Artur's there? Not me! I haven't even thought about the guy since he said he wanted me to be a princess and then

49

swam out of town. And I don't *want* to think about him, and I'll thank you two to stop cramming him down my throat!"

Jonas and Moon blinked at her.

Fred coughed and lowered her voice. "Also, I'd like to use Sam's office for a minute. And also the bathroom. And then we're out of here."

"Well, that's fine, sweetie. Have fun at your Pelican."

"Oh, sure," Fred muttered. "Tons of fun at the Pelican. Pelican, here I come."

"Here *we* come," Jonas corrected her, cheerfully.

Fred bit back several retorts, contented herself with a final baleful glare, and exited the kitchen.

Seven

🌊

The van pulled up to the Pirate's Cove Resort on Little Cayman Island with its engine laboring. It was painted serial killer green, and smelled like feet.

"Finally!" Jonas said, peering out a dirty window. "I thought we'd never get here."

"And I thought you'd never shut up." It had been an excruciating twelve hours, made more difficult by the fact that Fred was not a fan of flying. But she only had herself to blame for the long day. She had declined the Grim Duo's offers to lead her to the meeting place via the ocean. She didn't think she could swim all the way to the Caymans in less than four days. In fact, she'd never been farther south than Florida. And she sure as hell couldn't keep up with a couple of full-blooded Undersea Folk. She'd pass on the humiliation, thanks.

As he had promised, Jonas had fixed her time off with Dr. Barb. He'd even packed their bags and cleaned out their fridges. Fred just sat back and let him organize her life. It made things easier on her, and seemed to calm him down.

She and Jonas climbed out of the van, fetched their luggage, then coughed as the driver roared off in a spume of dust.

"Real friendly around here, aren't they?" Jonas gasped, waving the cloud of dust away from his face.

"Well, we were promised privacy. Can't have mermaids beaching themselves on public property."

Jonas snickered and slung his bag over one shoulder. He was bizarrely attired in a yellow Hawaiian shirt, buttercup yellow shorts, and penny loafers without socks. He had forgotten his sunglasses, and so he squinted. His hair, as always, looked perfect.

Fred, by contrast, felt as wrung out as an old washcloth. Her green hair was matted to her head, she needed a shower, and her shorts kept trying to climb into her ass. If she actually cared about her appearance, this could be—

"Hey! You're here!"

And before she could say anything, or step out of reach, Dr. Thomas Pearson ran up to her and planted a kiss on her mouth.

Eight

"Wh-what?" She dropped her bag. On her foot, unfortunately, but she was too amazed to reach for her throbbing toes. "What are you doing here?"

"You kidding? Who do you think is paying for the resort?" Thomas spread his arms, indicating the deserted buildings and empty beach. "I promised Artur I'd clear out the resort so you guys could have your big meeting. Booked the whole place for a month and gave the staff paid time off. Bad news is, we have to do our own cooking."

"You *know* about the Pelagic?"

Her fellow marine biologist laughed hard. "Yeah, is that a great name, or what?"

"I don't get it," Jonas complained. "Stop talking in your secret marine biologist language, you geeks. But it's nice to see you again, Dr. Moneybags."

"You, too, Jonas." The two men shook hands. "You still seeing Barb?"

"Ohhhh, yes!"

"Don't get him started," Fred begged.

She made a mighty effort to recover from her shock. As if the upcoming Pelagic wasn't unnerving enough, as if the Grim Duo hadn't been annoying, now here was Thomas, friendly as a puppy and ten times as cute. Her mouth actually burned from his kiss.

She tried again. "What are you doing here?"

He slung an arm around her and she shook him off. "You've only got yourself to blame," he said cheerfully. "Artur tracked me down in England and invited me to the meeting. Apparently it's bad form among mer-people to pursue a lady while fixing it so your rival *can't*."

"What?" Fred was having a terrible time tracking the conversation.

"Oh ho!" Jonas cried, and she was annoyed to see

that her friend was having zero trouble tracking the conversation. "Artur won't try to get Fred into bed unless you're also trying?"

"Basically."

"*What?*"

Jonas cringed away from her, but Thomas, to his credit, stood his ground. "Who am I to argue with Undersea Folk tradition?"

"I think I could take a crack at it," Fred retorted.

"Hey, it's actually pretty civilized when you think about it."

"Too bad," she grated, "no one ran it by me."

"Besides, you think I'd miss this chance? No way in hell!"

"The chance to try to bone Fred?" Jonas asked, wiggling his blond brows. "Or to see a thousand topless mermaids?"

"Whatever." Thomas beamed. "It's all good."

"I'm getting a migraine," Fred muttered. "Which hut is mine?"

"The one I'm sleeping in," Thomas said hopefully.

"Nice try. I'll take that one." And she marched toward number six.

Nine

The insistent banging on her hut door woke Fred from an uneasy nap. In fact, at first the pounding incorporated itself into her dream.

It was thirty years ago and she was trying to break into her mother's house to warn her not not *not* to have sex with the merman she found on the beach. But no matter how hard she pounded, her mother didn't heed, or even turn her head. Fred pounded harder—

—and woke up.

Her door was actually rattling on the hinges; whoever

was outside was in a hell of a hurry to talk to her (or possibly to use her bathroom). She rolled off the bed and staggered to the door.

"All right, hold your pee!" She yanked the door open and felt herself seized, lifted off her feet, and squeezed in a mighty bear hug.

She punched the Prince of the Undersea Folk in his left eye, and he set her down. "Ah, my Rika. How nice to see you again." He touched his eye, which was starting to swell. "As gracious as ever."

"That's what you get, Grabby Pants." She tried to sound grudging, but was quite pleased to see him again. And he looked wonderful, as always. Big. Vibrant. Hair and beard those unbelievable shades of red. Like King Neptune in the flesh. And speaking of flesh, he was clothed (barely) in a pair of tattered khaki shorts and that was it. He wiggled his sand-covered toes in her direction. "What's the big rush?"

"Only to see you, Little Rika. I am pleased you accepted our invitation."

"The Grim Duo didn't make it sound like I had much choice."

"Grim?" Artur's kingly brow furrowed, then smoothed. "Ah, Tennian and that other fellow, what's-his-name."

"Comforting that you can't remember them all, either. Anyway, they sort of goose-stepped me until I showed up."

Artur threw his head back and laughed. "As if anyone could force your hand, Fredrika Bimm!"

"I think that was a compliment."

He beamed at her. "And how is your lady mother?"

"She's great. She and my stepdad have started taking in foster kids."

Artur's brow wrinkled. "Foster . . . ?"

"Kids whose parents beat on them or are orphans or whatever."

"Your people . . . *beat* children? *Your own children?*"

"Well." She coughed. "Yeah. Some of them. Us."

Artur made a mighty effort and managed to clear the look of horror from his face. "Well, that is a fine thing your mother does. A great lady."

"Thanks. You're looking good." Mild understatement.

"And you, Little Rika, *you* look good enough to gobble up raw."

"How sweet. You want to explain what Thomas is doing here?"

Artur scowled, and Fred barely swallowed the giggle that tried to escape. "He is my chief rival for your affections."

"Yeah, okay, keep going."

"It would be unseemly to whisk you away somewhere he could not access. I must show every courtesy to my rival. Also," Artur added thoughtfully, "I wish for my father to meet him. He is a formidable warrior. For a biped."

"So you said last year."

"Ah, your wound." He poked her shoulder, and she restrained the urge to punch him in the other eye. These people had no sense of personal space. "You have healed well?"

"Sure. No thanks to you two psychos."

"You cannot fault our concern."

There was plenty she could fault them with. But now wasn't the time. "Well, brace yourself. Not only is Thomas here, but you're stuck with Jonas, too. He sort of came with the package."

Artur didn't smile, but he didn't freak out, either. "Your friend has behaved honorably in the past, and has kept your secret for . . . what?"

"Going on twenty-five years."

"I do not fear Jonas; he is discreet."

"Discreet? You must be thinking of another Jonas."

"It was good that Thomas accepted my invitation," Artur continued. "He and Jonas will be the first surface dwellers in the history of our kind to come to a Pelagic."

"Yeah, and it's all gone straight to his head."

"That would be because of your presence, Little Rika, not mine."

"Ha," she said sourly. "And speaking of my presence, you want to explain why it was so hot-damn important for me to come to your meeting?"

"Ah . . . yes. But later. Have you dined?"

"I had some Pringles on one of the planes."

"I do not know what a Pringle is, but it sounds vile. Come." He held out a large hand, and she took it. Her own paw was swallowed in an instant. She sensed rather than felt the crushing power held in check. She was strong, but Artur was a redheaded Superman. "We will eat."

"Don't think I don't know I'm getting the runaround on this Pelagic thing," she warned him as he practically dragged her out the door. "I keep asking and people keep blowing me off."

Artur beamed at her. "We have grouper."

Ten

Artur led her past the swimming pool to the main hut—the lodge, in other words—which had the largest bar she'd ever seen. The thing was the size of her living room, and at least twenty of the bottles were rum. And, like her home, it was set up as one big room . . . the bar led into the cocktail lounge, which led into the dining room, which led into the kitchen. All tastefully decorated with plastic dolls strung up in' fishnets. Sort of an *Alice in Wonderland* meets *CSI* crime scene look.

Supper had been set up buffet style and Fred didn't

hesitate to dig in. Thomas had warned there wasn't a cook, but someone was sure doing a great job with the kitchen. She had been so hungry she'd forgotten she was hungry—funny how that happened sometimes—but the minute she had smelled the savory grilled vegetables she'd started drooling like a hyena.

As she dished up salad and vegetables, the only other diners—Jonas and Thomas—raised hands in greeting. Jonas quit eating his grouper long enough to lope over to the bar, fix her a vodka sour, and lope back. He plunked the glass down in front of her and went back to shoveling in fish.

"Thanks. Where is everybody?" she asked as she and Artur sat across from them. She glanced out the large windows and saw what she had seen when the van dropped them off: absolutely nothing and no one.

"Mmmph," Jonas replied.

"Oh, they're around here somewhere," Thomas said with a calculated vagueness that didn't fool Fred. No way would a mermaid geek *not* know where at least a few of the Undersea Folk were.

"Eat your salad," was Artur's answer.

If she hadn't been so hungry, she'd have firmly

plonked her fork on the table as a dramatic attention-getting device and refused to pick it up again until she had answers. As it was, she barely had enough time between forkfuls to mumble, "What's going on? What are you guys hiding? Badly?"

"Eat your asparagus," Jonas replied.

"Who's hiding?" Thomas asked, looking guilty.

Artur loudly cleared his throat, a noise that sounded like a cement truck going up a gravelly hill in low gear. "What do you bipeds call this?"

"We call it strawberry pie," Fred answered. "And seriously, this changing the subject thing . . . You guys are terrible at this."

"So, my new book debuted at number twenty-six on the *USA Today* list," Thomas remarked, scraping his plate.

"I assume you bring up such a thing to garner praise?" Artur asked.

"Yeah, he's garnering," Jonas said, draining his rum and Coke. "That means a bunch of bipeds bought his tree-murdering book."

"Well, jeez, when you put it that way," Thomas mumbled, crestfallen, and Fred snorted into her drink.

"It's a good thing," Jonas finished, quoting one of his idols, Martha Stewart. He still maintained she'd been framed by the bigwigs at Enron to take the heat off themselves. "That's part of the reason he was able to fix it so we'd have this whole resort to ourselves."

"Yes, and although my lord father gave thanks, I myself have not done so yet," Artur pointed out. "We are not without funds, and if you do not mind being compensated in gold, we can—"

Thomas started to demur, when Fred interrupted. "You've met the king?" she gasped. "*I* haven't even met the king!"

"Well, you should," Thomas said, trying (and failing) not to sound smug. "He's a great guy. Managed not to vomit at the thought of a disgusting surface dweller muddying up his Pelagic."

"What's he look like?" Jonas asked.

Thomas pointed his fork at the prince. "Picture Artur here in another thirty years."

"I do not think we count time the same way," Artur said, pausing before demolishing his third piece of pie. "My lord father had sixty-two years when I was born."

Fred and the bipeds—err, her friends—gaped at the prince. "You—what? Seriously?" she asked.

"We have discussed this before," Artur said mildly, his princely aura dimmed by the glob of strawberry preserves on his upper lip. "Undersea Folk live longer and age slower."

"And are super strong and have gorgeous coloring and gravity is kind to them because they don't need bras," Jonas said in one breath. "At least, the two mermaids I've seen—Fred and Tennian—sure don't."

"Gosh, I'm all atwitter." She chewed furiously on a broccoli head. "And speaking for Tennian, mutter, mumble, mumble."

"Hey, they can't all be as charming and warmhearted as you," Jonas said, leaning forward and spearing a baby carrot off her plate.

"Are you talking about that gorgeous blue-haired girl?" Thomas asked, visibly surprised. "Don't knock her, you horrible woman. She's sweet."

"How can you tell? She never raises her voice. I don't even think she has teeth. You know those people who are so quiet they make me nervous? I was actually wishing one of *those* was in my apartment at the time. She doesn't talk!"

"As opposed to some of my folk, who continually speak," Artur teased. "And of course she has teeth. You should see her in a school of shrimp."

"Is today 'shit on Fred and steal her food' day?" she demanded. "Because nobody told me."

"My lord father is coming a-land tonight and would like to see you then," Artur explained. "Right now he is dining with some council members."

"Hey, you got out of a state dinner," Jonas pointed out.

"Yes, and I have my biped friends and Little Rika to thank for it."

"Gee," Thomas said, coughing into his napkin. "That gets me right here."

"I'm thinking about getting you right there," Fred warned, waving her fork threateningly. "So where is everybody?"

All three spoke in unison:

"Eating."

"Sleeping."

"Exploring."

Fred sighed into the embarrassed silence. "Well? Which is it?"

"Well, first they ate, and then they took naps . . ." Jonas was clearly making it up as he went along. "Then they, um, explored. Because there's all kinds of stuff to explore here. In the Caymans."

"Undersea trenches and such," Thomas added, trying to help Jonas.

"You guys. It's just so sad. I'm embarrassed for you, I really am." She savagely chewed a final asparagus tip, swallowed, and added, "Fine, don't tell me. But I'm gonna find out." She shook her head and got up to get a slice of pie.

Eleven

After dinner, Artur and Jonas disappeared somewhere—it was still light, and Jonas wanted to get in some snorkeling while he could. So he took off in the direction of the equipment shed, while Artur went to check on his dad. Which left Thomas and Fred walking on the beach.

"I've got to give this place credit," Fred said, peering at the horizon. "Being here is like being trapped in the Discovery Channel."

"I assume you meant that in a nice way."

"Of course. What other way would I mean it?"

"Hard to tell with you."

They walked in silence for a few seconds, until Fred couldn't bear the quiet another moment and blurted, "I was really surprised to see you today."

His teeth were a white flash in the near dark. "Excellent."

"Well, I was."

"Yeah, well. Think I was going to miss this? The Pelagic? *And* the chance to see you again?"

She stopped walking and, after a moment, he noticed and came back to stand beside her. "You had a year to see me again," she pointed out. "And you didn't."

He shifted his feet in the sand, but didn't break her gaze. "I had projects. Work to finish. I couldn't just show up on your doorstep playing a guitar and serenading you until you agreed to go out with me."

Why not? She shook the odd and unworthy thought aside. "Yeah, but an e-mail? A postcard?"

"We're here now, Fred. Together."

She barked laughter. "Oh, sure. You, me, Jonas, Artur, and ten thousand mermaids. Not that any of them have bothered to come ashore. And don't think I didn't notice."

"It's . . . complicated, Fred. It's—"

"Never mind. I just—"

"What?"

Missed you. Thought about you all the time. Wished you would have come sooner. But she could say none of those things to Thomas without also saying them to Artur. And that was the worst kind of unfair. "I just think it's weird, how we're all together again for this meeting," she improvised.

"Tell me about it. But I've been prepping for the meeting, and I've got something to show you. See that?" Thomas pointed to what appeared to be a float anchored several yards out. "You up for swimming out there?"

"Up for it? I haven't been wet in two days." The double entendre made the color rush to her face and she ignored Thomas's grin. "Not to mention, I'll get out there five times faster than you will."

"Great." Thomas was pulling his shirt over his head and kicking off his shoes. "Then I'll see you out there."

"And we're swimming out there *why*?" she called after him as he scampered into the surf.

"Like I said, I've got something to show you!" he shouted over his shoulder, and then dived in.

"Yeah, well. I'm a scientist. Chances are I've seen it already," she muttered, but waded in after him, stripping off her clothes as she went and tossing them back toward the beach.

Twelve

She floundered clumsily in the surf for a few seconds until it was deep enough for her to shift to her tail-form. Then she was able to go from fighting the water to being part of it.

At first she just stretched her muscles and gloried in being able to get some decent exercise for the first time in too long. Then, as the sand floor dropped away from her, she was able to take a good look around and really appreciate her surroundings.

In just the short distance to the float, she saw at least

forty different species of fish. It was astonishing. She was very much afraid she was swimming around like a tourist, with her eyes bulging and her mouth hanging open.

And the water was delightful—warm and clear. She almost didn't mind swimming in the ocean if it was like this. (Almost.) As opposed to back home, where the Atlantic was chilly and murky, and hid unpleasant surprises.

Here she could see everything coming—sea turtles, manta rays, sharks, angelfish. She could hear their fish-chatter whispering in the back of her brain, a far cry from the hectoring nagging of the fish at the New England Aquarium, who often went on strike to get what they wanted.

And the sand! It looked like sugar, pure and perfect and gorgeous. It was almost possible to believe they hadn't wrecked the planet if there were still places like this left.

She had passed Thomas almost at once and now circled the float, waiting for him. She stroked a sea turtle as it paddled past her. It snootily ignored her and paddled away.

She laughed, causing a stream of bubbles, and nearly crashed into the underwater ladder when she saw the surprise.

It was a small submarine, but unlike any sub she had ever seen. It was sleek and shiny, and had more windows per square foot than metal, or so it seemed at first glance.

It was obviously brand-new; no barnacles, no clinging seaweed. So the bobbing rectangle above wasn't a float; it was a marker for this little sub, and a way for people to climb down and—

Thomas had finally reached her, gone up for a big breath, then swam back down. He motioned to her (she assumed . . . who else would he be gesturing to?), opened the air lock, and swam in. She was right behind him, consumed with curiosity and delight.

He shut the air lock door, drained the water, and grinned at her. "Ready for the nickel tour?" he said, raising his voice to be heard over the pumps.

"You've been busy the last few months," she commented, trying to hide how impressed she was.

"Well, duh. I don't spend all my money on bookmarks and renting resorts, y'know. Come on."

She followed him in.

Thirteen

It wasn't so much a submarine, Thomas explained, as an underwater RV, complete with tiny kitchen, shower, and bedroom. And it was far more comfortable than any submarine she'd ever seen. And . . .

She took a deep, appreciative whiff. "Ah, that new car smell!" She covered her nudity with a towel and rubbed her hair with another one. "Just like you drove it off the lot!"

"Yup." It hadn't taken him long to show her around the underwater RV, or URV (pronounced "Irv"), as he called it. Everything was miniaturized (even the bed . . . bigger than a twin, not quite as big as a double) and brand-spanking-new. And everything was state of the art. "I brought along a bunch of DVDs, the galley's stocked, and as long as you don't mind saltwater showers, the bathroom's all yours."

"Thanks."

He shuffled his feet awkwardly, looking more like a sixteen-year-old than the formidable (and full-grown) Dr. Thomas Pearson. "I mean, I know you've got your hut on the beach, and you've got the run of the ocean, but if you ever want to, you know, get some space or retreat from a couple hundred Undersea Folk, you're always welcome in the URV."

"Well. Thanks." Fred wasn't quite sure how to respond to that. It was a generous offer . . . unless it was all part of his plan to get into her pants, in which case it was vile and underhanded. So she should either give him a sisterly hug, or punch him in the face. What to do, what to do . . .

She coughed. "How long did this take to make?"

"Well, I had the plans for a few months—I designed them after I went to Scotland last year."

She remembered; it had been the last stop on his fellowship. They'd defeated the bad guy, both he and Artur had declared their love, and then both of them had *left*—Artur to go back to the Black Sea and do whatever it was princes did; Thomas to finish his fellowship.

"When Artur got in touch, I had the URV built." He lowered his voice, although the two of them were the only ones in the URV. "I was just waiting for an excuse, you know? I've been fantasizing about the URV since I was a kid."

Uh-huh. Not *too* disturbing. "He's a marine biologist, he's an M.D., he writes books, he's rich, and he designs underwater love nests. Is there anything he can't do?"

"Well, I can't talk about myself in the third person without creeping myself out, so knock it off."

"Wait a minute, wait a minute." Fred frowned, thinking about it. "So this Pelagic . . . The Folk have known about it for at least a few months?"

"Yeah, I guess. Well. The royal family did, anyway. Who knows when Artur and his dad told everybody else."

"Hmm."

"I'm just jazzed they even invited me, y'know?"

"Yes. Can't blame you for that one at all. I'm kind of jazzed myself."

"Like you wouldn't be invited."

"Some half-breed loser who was raised by vicious, bloodthirsty bipeds?" She smiled grimly at his stricken expression. "Right, you and I know that's not the case, but they don't, and like I said, I'm glad to be invited. I s'pose." She sought to change the subject, and so looked the URV up and down and all around. "I'll bet you've got cameras set up all over the—"

"Well, sure. Among other things, the URV is a portable television studio. Lights, sound, picture—it's got—"

"But you know Artur and his dad—not to mention the other eighty thousand Undersea Folk—aren't going to let you put this footage on CNN."

"No," Thomas admitted, "but I couldn't pass up the chance to film, even if it just stays in my own library. Besides, it's going to be helpful for my next book."

"*The Mermaid and the Milkman*?"

"*The Anatomy and Physiology of Homo Nautilus*," he retorted stiffly. "You gotta admit, with my background, I'm in a pretty good position to write that book." It was true; Thomas was not only a Ph.D., he was an

M.D. "And if they 'come out' to the world, so to speak, we're going to have to know how to take care of them. My book could be in every hospital, every med school, every medical library in the world."

She didn't even try to hold back her laughter. "*Homo Nautilus?*"

"Also known as the Undersea Folk, and stop laughing, you rotten bitch."

With a mighty effort, she got herself under control. "Yeah, but what if they decide to stay put?"

Thomas shrugged. "Then the manuscript stays on the shelf and my tapes stay in the URV and nobody has to know. I'll respect their decision."

"You will unless you want Artur kicking your balls up into your throat."

"Like I'm scared of *him*," he sneered. Fred had to admit he was entitled to his fearlessness; there had been a throw-down between the two of them last fall, and Thomas had held his own. A good trick, given that Artur was bigger, heavier, and probably three times as strong.

Then he shrugged. "I'm looking on the bright side. If they do decide to come forward, I'm perfectly positioned. If they don't, it was still a once-in-a-lifetime experience. Well worth the time." He leered at her. "On several levels."

"Pig. And Artur and his dad know all about this. The taping you're doing for the Discovery Channel, I mean."

Thomas coughed. "No. They don't. And I'd appreciate it if you kept it to yourself for now, Fred. If it comes to it, of course I'll let them in on my project, but for now there's no point in saying anything."

"Knock yourself out, Mermaid Geek. Just keep me out of it."

Thomas slowly shook his head. "Not this time, Fred. This time, like it or not, you're *in* it. In fact, you're practically the guest of honor."

"Sure," she snapped. "That explains why none of the purebloods want to be around me except Artur, and he's got brain damage."

Thomas flushed, but didn't look away.

"So what's going on?" she demanded. "Why are they keeping their distance?"

"Well." Thomas cleared his throat. "I'm not sure it's for me to say."

"You'd *better* say."

"It's kind of private Undersea Folk business."

"But *you* know it? Forget it, Thomas. Cough up, or cough up blood."

"Okay, okay, I'm not up to taking a punch, so just relax. Here, have a seat."

She let him steer her to one of the narrow bar stools in the galley. "Okay. So what's going on?"

"Well, I can't just blurt it out."

"You'd better!"

"I'm just saying, there's background, there's stuff to cover. Okay. So, it's like this. See, your fath—"

There was a click, and the intercom system came to life. "Ho inside, Thomas!" Artur's booming voice. "My father and I require entrance!"

"Hit the red button and come on in," Thomas called. He shrugged apologetically at Fred. "I guess we'll talk about that later. But now you get to meet the king."

"Oh, goody."

Fourteen

Artur and an older, craggier version of Artur stepped out of the air lock and into the URV. "Ah, Thomas," Older, Craggier Artur boomed, not noticing (or not caring) that he and Artur were dripping water all over the galley. "Do you have more movie-shows of the great warrior Al Swearengen for me to view?"

"Sure, King Mekkam. Season two is all set to go."

Al Swearengen? Now why did that sound so—

"And this must be Fredrika, the spirited beauty who has my good son twisted so far around he can see the back of his own tail." The king pulled Fred into a rib-shattering hug and she groaned. He pushed her back, beaming. Clearly his father had no more clue about personal space than Artur did. Very grabby, the Undersea Folk. "It is a great delight to meet you at last, Fredrika. And how is your lady mother?"

"Mom's fine," she gasped. Awfully worried about blood relatives, these guys. Artur *always* asked about her mom, though he'd only met her the one time. And the king, she was certain, had never met Moon. "I'm fine." This was a rather large lie. "We're all fine. Nice to meet you, too. Thanks for inviting me to your Pelagic."

"Oh, no. Indeed, no." King Mekkam frowned, and Fred realized that Thomas had described him perfectly. He really did look like an older, grayer version of Artur. They were even the same height.

They were also naked, but Fred was trying not to let that bother her. After all, they couldn't teleport to the URV, now could they? No. They had to swim, and the best way for a merman to swim was *not* layered down with Lands' End apparel.

And she had to face facts. Despite the efforts of her hippie mother, Fred was uncomfortable because of the repressed sexual mores of a society that had been heavily influenced by the Victorian Age. Her father's people, of course, had no idea who Queen Victoria even was, much less why they should be embarrassed to walk around with their dicks swinging—

"No, it is I who must thank you," the king was saying. "It was kind of you to join us on such short notice. I am not unaware that you had to disrupt your life and your plans to come to our meeting. And for your friend to come as well! You do my people such an honor as they have never been done before. And that is excellent," he added, almost muttered.

"Yeah, King Mekkam, that's great, listen—maybe you can explain how—"

"*Deadwood*, season two," Thomas announced, waving the box at the king, who nearly swooned like a girl with a crush.

"Excellent! Oh, that is excellent, Thomas, thank you! Do you know of this movie-show?" the king demanded, snatching the season two DVD set out of Thomas's hand.

"Uh . . . yeah, I heard about it. Mostly the uproar when HBO decided to cancel—"

Mekkam steamrolled right over her. "The hero is a treacherous, aging warrior named Al Swearengen. He is as perfidious a biped as I have ever seen, and he is the king of Deadwood. He has many enemies and triumphs with a combination of violence and deception." The king said this with total admiration.

"You've got him watching *Deadwood*?" Fred hissed, twisting Thomas's ear until he yelped. "*That's* the part of human culture you decided to expose him to?"

"It wasn't my fault! I had it on when I was giving these guys the tour."

"Now, unless you motherfuckers are going to join me," King Mekkam continued, "I insist you sons of bastards all be quiet so I may view more of King Al."

Fred groaned.

"Uh, King Mekkam, about the swearing," Thomas said, clearing his throat and rubbing his ear. "I'm not quite sure you've got the hang of it just yet, and—"

"In our culture, it is polite to speak to others in their dialect," the king said firmly. "So all you motherfuckers shut the fuck up. Now, Thomas. Where is your son of a bitching DVD machine?"

"Oh man, oh man, oh man."

"You're going to hell for this one," Fred told him. "If nothing else."

"And do you have any motherfucking potato chips?"

Fifteen

🦄

The next day, Fred found out why her father's people were going out of their way to avoid her, no thanks to Thomas, Jonas, or Artur. Naturally.

On the whole, she would have preferred to remain in ignorance. Not that the Terrible Trio had any right to keep it from her. But she sort of understood their reasoning. Sort of.

She had gotten up early, had oatmeal with milk and cane sugar, then gone for an early morning swim. The sun had just started peeking over the horizon and no one else was stirring. Fred was not normally an early riser, but the night before she hadn't slept for shit.

Stress, she decided. Nerves. Because God knew she'd been exhausted after all the traveling and should have slept like a dead thing. Still, she figured she clocked in maybe two, three hours, max. Depending on when the Pelagic started, hopefully she could sneak in a nap.

Anyway, come sunrise she'd been wide awake. Some kind person had laid out oatmeal, cold cereals, bacon, a variety of juices, and ice-cold milk. She'd bolted a quick breakfast alone, and then headed out.

She swam past the URV into deeper water, curious to see what other varieties of marine life were out and about at this ungodly hour, and had stroked a manta ray. (They were so silky she was always amazed . . . They were like giant mushrooms with eyes.) That was when she saw him.

He was lean, as most of her father's people seemed to be, almost too thin. She could count his ribs, even twenty feet away as she was. Due to the glorious clarity of the water she could see him perfectly, even through schools of darting fish.

His hair was the same startling blue as Tennian's; his

eyes the same shade of dark blue—almost black. His long, broad tail was a thousand shades of green, the colors so vivid they were almost hypnotic, rather like a peacock's tail.

Her tail, in contrast, was shorter and narrower. And it had as much blue as green in it. Full-blooded Undersea Folk were superior swimmers, of course, and stronger than she was. That had been difficult to get used to. Before meeting Artur, she had prided herself on being one of the fastest things in the ocean.

Ha! Not anymore. Not hardly.

I'm staring, she thought, embarrassed. Too late to cover it now. Better say something.

Morning, she thought at him.

Without a word, he turned around and began swimming away.

Hey. HEY! I'm talking to you! Thinking at you, anyway. She darted after him with a flex of her tail. *What, did I get the super secret mermaid handshake wrong?*

I do not wish to be seen with traitor's kin, he replied, not even turning around. In fact, he was rapidly putting distance between them.

Traitor's what? Hey! Get your fishy ass back here!

Please forgive my brother, a new voice thought. *He frets about his reputation so.*

Startled, she whipped around to see Tennian swimming up on her blind side. *You!*

Me, she agreed. *Good morning.*

Morning. He didn't even like me! Don't misunderstand; I'm used to it. She folded her fist under her chin, thinking. *But he didn't even* know *me. Usually people have to be around me for at least half an hour before they decide I'm a jerk.*

Sometimes, Tennian added without cracking a smile, *much less than half an hour.*

You're way more talkative underwater, anybody ever tell you?

No. Tennian was now swimming in slow, lazy circles around Fred. *I am not comfortable with outlander styles of speech. It hurts my throat, though courtesy dictates we try. But I do not have to vocalize now.*

Uh-huh, great, good, fine, and while we're chatting here, what the hell was your brother bitching about? And is he your twin or something? He looks just like you, although he could use a protein shake.

We were born of the same mother at the same time, yes.

92

Fred was beginning to have a sinking idea what Tennian's stiff-ass brother had been complaining about. God knew nobody ever talked about her father.

Her mother never talked about him, of course, because they'd only been together the one night. Fred had known by the time she was five that her mother didn't know a damned thing about her dad . . . not even that he'd been a merman. Moon Bimm only put two and two together when she was bathing the newborn Fred at home . . . and her green-haired baby had popped a tail, right there in the baby tub.

But the other Undersea Folk Fred had met? They hadn't talked about him, either. Which was weird, if you thought about it. *None* of them thought she might want to know about her birth dad? Or if they did, felt they couldn't discuss him? But why?

It could only be because he'd done something fairly horrid. And what had stiff-ass said? Or thought?

I do not wish to be seen with traitor's kin. Yeah. That was it.

Fred sighed internally, then braced herself. *All right. Hit me.*

She could feel Tennian's surprise, and hastily added,

Tell me what he did. Better yet, tell me about the last time a Pelagic was held. You and Kertal got a little squir-relly in my apartment when I was asking questions about it, so cough up.

She sensed Tennian trying to decipher Fred's slang, and realized one advantage telepathy had over verbal communication was that even if you didn't understand the other person's exact words, you at least got their meaning.

Tennian blew out a breath, making a stream of bubbles that startled a wrasse into darting away, and seemed to be thinking hard about how to begin.

Finally: *Your father, Kortrim, felt that good King Mekkam's family had been in power quite long enough. Six generations . . . and seven, once Mekkam is no more and Artur is king. And Kortrim was able to talk many of the young ones into assisting him, ones bored with our hidden life and hungry for more power.*

Palace coup, eh? Fucking great.

Sixteen

Fred was still trying to grasp the idea that her father, whom she'd never much thought about, had been a traitor. Someone who had tried to overthrow Mekkam and his whole family. Someone who likely would have *killed* Mekkam, Artur, and the rest of the royals.

The thought made her heart want to stop, but she forced herself to follow it to its logical conclusion.

Yes, of course her dad would have executed Artur and the others. He would have had to. Rule number one after a hostile takeover: get rid of the old guard.

I cannot believe, she thought, and hoped the thought was private, *that I'm descended from a murderous betraying asshole.* The asshole part? Not such a surprise. The betraying murdering part? Ugh. She tried to imagine the circumstances which would lead her to try to get Dr. Barb fired behind her back (or even to her face) . . . and hit a blank wall.

She and Tennian were floating rather than swimming, letting the current take them back to shore. Fred impatiently batted a grouper aside. *So in your tactful way, you're telling me that Dear Old Dad tried to overthrow the monarchy.*

Yes.

What was his beef with Artur's dad?

She could sense Tennian's hesitation and added, *Well, fer Crissakes, don't stop now!*

Your sire felt that the accident of birth enjoyed by the king's line was no reason to keep a crown.

Huh?

His mind-touch.

Whose? Fred was utterly mystified. *Mekkam's? Or Artur's?*

Both. All.

Mind-touch? All right, this is clearly a cultural thing, so Fred would decipher that later. *Never mind. Obviously Dear Old Dad failed, otherwise he'd be King Dear Old Dad and I'd be Princess Fred.* Now that was a laugh!

And may be still.

What?

Yes. He failed. In fact, many of those he thought he had brought to his side were only pretending so they could report his duplicity to the king.

So the betrayer got betrayed. Okay, that's interesting. I guess. Actually, there's a kind of elegant irony to it. So, what? They killed him?

Oh, no! Fred felt real shock behind Tennian's horrified thought. *We never. We NEVER. We are not like surface dwellers, to take life so lightly!*

All right, all right, calm down. Fred decided it wasn't a good time to remind the younger woman that she was half–surface dweller. *So if they didn't kill him, and if he isn't here, then where . . . ?*

Banishment. The thought was as flat as a sugar cookie, but not nearly as sweet. *It is our most severe punishment.*

I bet.

The ocean is vast. And I do not have to tell you how dangerous it can be. It is . . . a difficult place to face alone. It is one thing to go off by yourself for a day or two, but for the rest of your life? And our kind are much, much longer lived than your mother's.

Fred was feeling pretty horrified herself, and tried to keep it from Tennian. No sense in scaring the girl into clamming up again.

She tried to imagine living in the sea her whole life, only to be cast out by everyone she had ever known. Water covered three-fourths of the planet; it would be beyond awful to face all that alone.

Not for a year or two. Not for a decade or two. But for decade after decade after decade, leading into centuries, until . . . How long *was* the life span for an Undersea Folk, anyway?

Not to mention . . .

That's a good way to get killed, isn't it? Without the group to protect you, to look after you . . . I mean, he must have died. Artur was sure of it, or he wouldn't have told my mom he was prob'ly dead.

We think . . . but we do not know. No one ever saw

him again, and no one speaks of him. It was assumed,
once King Mekkam discovered your existence, that your
sire perhaps came ashore that very night and lay with
your lady mother. It was the last documented sighting
of him, at any rate.

Fred made a mental note to never, ever tell this to her
mother. Moon Bimm still had the hippie's romanticized
view of life, and The Night Fred Was Conceived was one
of her more cherished stories.

The mysterious stranger showing up on the beach.
Moon, tipsy on cheap wine, and lonely. The drunken
fuck (or, as Moon called it, "the tender, life-making
lovemaking"). Followed by five months of morning sick-
ness and, eventually, a mer-baby.

No, she'd never tell Moon that the only reason her
dad had come ashore was because his people had thrown
his ass out.

She also made a mental note to find out how, exactly,
Mekkam had learned of her existence. Because Artur
had alluded to that last fall, hadn't he? He'd told her,
while they were in her mother's kitchen at the Cape Cod
house, that his father had sent him to seek her out.

I'm getting it now! That's why no one spoke of it to

me. *Why everybody keeps dancing around my questions. Do they blame me for what my dad did? They must. But that doesn't make any sense . . . Anybody who knows I'm his kid also knows I never met the guy. So are they really that dumb?*

She'd been deliberately provocative (she didn't know any other way to be), but Tennian didn't rise to the bait.

Not . . . dumb, Fredrika. But family is all, to the Undersea Folk. Responsible for everything, the author of everything. We believe personality traits are passed down as easily as hair color and tail length. Some of us . . .

Reluctance now, extreme reluctance, and Tennian looked away from Fred, snatched a damselfish from the middle of its school, and disposed of it in four chomps. All this with the absent air of someone biting their fingernails. Fred struggled mightily not to barf. The blood didn't bother her; the casual carnivorousness did, not to mention the sight of Tennian's needle-sharp teeth. *Some of us believe that if your sire could act in such a treacherous way, so might you. But for the prince . . .*

What about Artur?

He is most fond of you. Surely, she added, waving away the blood and scales, *this is nothing new.*

Oh, he's babbled something along those lines. I wasn't paying much attention.

You may wish to. Fred could sense Tennian's dry amusement. *He has made no secret of the fact that he wishes to make you his princess. And but for that . . .*

Are you telling me if Artur wasn't sweet on me, nobody'd want me around?

I cannot tell you what might be, or might have been, Tennian said tactfully. *Only what is. Or was, if I have that knowledge.*

Fred floated for a few seconds, thinking. Then: *So your twin gave me the cold shoulder, but not you? How come? Not that I'm complaining. But nobody's come ashore since I got here. Except for Artur and the king and you, nobody's talked to me. I'm apparently the guest of honor, but nobody's even tried to look me up. So why are you being so friendly? Relatively speaking.*

I like your friend, Tennian said shyly. *The blond one. I never knew a surface dweller could be so loyal.*

The blond . . . Oh, Jonas! For God's sake. *Jonas* was why Tennian was breaking The Mermaid Code of Silence? He'd laugh his ass off when she told him. Assuming she decided his ego wouldn't go all Fourth of July from the stimulation.

His Highness says your friend has kept your secret for many years. For a surface dweller that would be accomplishment enough, but your friend is different.

You don't know HOW different.

As a man of science he could have gotten a great deal of gold if he had whispered the right thing into the right ear.

Jonas isn't a big fan of gold. He likes to play the stock market, when he's not raiding the racks at Nordstrom's.

Whatever he likes to play with, Tennian thought at her seriously, without the slightest flicker of a smile, *he does not do so with your reputation, or your life. I was . . . unaware of that quality in bipeds. It has made me wish to speak with them, when I never wanted to before.*

That's why you're talking to me? Because I've got good taste in friends?

Well, as they say, you cannot choose kin, only allies. And you chose well. It made me think you would be wise in other things as well. Oh, I am sorry! That was rude of me. Tennian used a tiny bone to pick her sharp, sharp teeth. *Did you want me to catch something for you?*

Good God no! Fred calmed herself as Tennian's eyes went wide in surprise at the vehemence of her tone. Thought. Whatever. *I mean, no thanks. I'm allergic.*

Allergic?

Fish makes me sick.

Fish . . . makes you ill?

Yeah, but don't worry. I eat plenty of vegetables, protein, stuff like that. Really, Tennian, don't worry.

It makes you ILL?

Well, remember, I'm only half Undersea Folk. Luckily, Mom and Sam were vegetarians, so it was never really a . . . Are you all right?

Then Tennian did something that amazed Fred: she laughed so hard she ended up upside down, her long blue hair actually dragging in the sand as she clutched her stomach and rolled back and forth in the current.

Ho ho ho, Tennian thought, rolling, rolling.

Fred watched her for a long moment, unamused. Finally: *You're an odd duck, Tennian.*

ILL? It makes you ILL? Ha! Ha! HA!

I could really, Fred added, *get to dislike you.*

Oh, I hope not, Tennian said, shaking sand out of her hair. *Because I think I will like you.*

You think you will like me? Fred was amused in spite of herself. Or, maybe, because of Tennian.

Oh yes! You and I will be great friends, I think. You will pretend I annoy you, while you secretly become more and more fond of me.

Think so?

Tennian put a small white hand out to Fred who, surprised, took it. *Of course. Because you are lonely, as am I. And lonely people have to stay close to one another. Do you not find that is so?*

And Fred, who disliked being cornered on any subject, couldn't help a nod of agreement.

Seventeen

§

I appreciate your laying all this out for me, Fred said. *God knows nobody else has said shit.*

You asked, Tennian replied simply. *How could I not answer?*

You'd be surprised how easily people haven't answered. Fred fumed and snorted to herself for a moment. *Not answering is not a problem at all for most people, seems like. So thanks.*

Courtesy to a guest is— What is THAT?

Fred looked. There, floating forty yards away, was

Thomas's pet project. *That's the URV. My—uh, my other biped friend, Thomas, he built it.*

It is so shiny! Like a shot, Tennian had crossed the forty yards and was swimming around and around the small silver URV. *So this is where the king keeps disappearing! We have been wondering and wondering, and to think, I, Tennian, have discovered the secret!*

Yeah. Good work.

Then this is Artur's rival for your affections, this Thomas.

Yeah.

Tennian stroked the shiny silver hull and looked up at Fred, dark blue eyes gleaming. *My people were positively humming at the thought of a half-bree—um, of a stranger attending the Pelagic. You can imagine our reaction when King Mekkam granted permission for a surface dweller to attend!*

Total freak-out, huh?

To put it mildly! But there was some concern as to how he was going to join us. Some thought he would have to bring air tanks and fins.

Right, a scuba suit.

Skooba?

Self-contained underwater breathing apparatus. Air tanks and fins. You've never heard that bef— Never mind. When would you have? Anyway, yeah, that was one option. But not very practical if you guys are going to be meeting for more than a couple of hours, which it sounds like you are.

Tennian had gone back to swimming in admiring circles. *He has built a little house for himself under the waves! How very, very clever!*

Why did Tennian's honest admiration make her uncomfortable? *Yeah, he's a clever guy.*

I knew of that quality in bipeds. But I did not know one could build something so aesthetically pleasing. It is not at all like those horrid clunky things that search for other war makers.

And, clear as thought, the image of a nuclear submarine left Tennian's mind and popped into Fred's. *That's a submarine, although war maker is as good a name as any. And you should see the inside of a Burger King if you think this is cool.*

Tennian was now pressing her face against one of the

windows and tapping her long fingers on the glass. Except it probably wasn't glass; it was probably some kind of durable—

He sees me! He is waving!

Of course, Fred thought sourly. *Why am I not surprised he's in there?* He's probably finding some other inappropriate HBO series for Mekkam to practice his vocabulary on. *The Sopranos,* maybe? *Entourage?* Oh, the horror.

Yeah, he's spending a lot of time in the URV.

He is beckoning for me to come in! May I?

What do I care?

It is allowed?

Fred nearly swam into the URV's smooth, curved corner. *You're asking* me?

Well. Tennian looked up at her. *He is unmated and you are unmated. So that is acceptable. But His Highness the prince has explained that this biped also wishes to make you his, so I—*

Tennian. We're just friends. He wants more, and I'm dealing with that. This felt like "not quite the truth," and Fred tried to shrug off her unease.

Not very well, as it clearly communicated to Tennian, who was frowning and keeping her distance. *But—*

Go.

Are you sure I will cause no offense?

My God, Fred thought. *I'm going to have to physically shove her into the URV or she'll think I'm in love with Thomas.*

I'm sure! Go!

Still, Tennian hesitated. *I think that you are being kind.*

Then you haven't been paying attention AT ALL.

I think that if I go in I will cause offense. I will stay out here, with you.

Tennian! I think it's physically impossible for you to cause offense. Come on, I'll introduce you.

You will? There will be a formal introduction?

Well, I don't know about formal—

I may go inside? It's permitted?

For God's sake. Come on.

Much later, Fred would come to bitterly regret that impulse. But for now, she was relieved (she was pretty sure) to see Tennian dart toward the air lock.

Eighteen

[seahorse illustration]

"Thomas, this is Tennian. Tennian, this is Dr. Thomas Pearson."

"It is good to meet you, Thomas."

"You, too, Tennian."

"That reminds me . . . I noticed you guys don't use last names. Do you even have them?"

"Last . . ." Tennian had been looking eagerly around the URV, but managed to wrench her attention back to Fred. "Oh, you mean family names! We have them—I am Tennian of the Meerklet line; and Artur, like his siblings and his father, are of the Zennor line—but we do not use them."

"Why not?" Thomas asked.

"Because . . . because we do not. It is not necessary. Normally," Tennian added, staring with big adoring eyes at the coffeemaker in the galley.

"Oh. Thanks for clearing that up." Fred cleared her throat. "Usually among bipeds, you don't call someone by their first name unless they ask you to, or you've known them for a while."

Tennian actually gasped in horror. "Then I have given offense!"

"No," Thomas breathed. "Not at all."

"Yeah," Fred said sourly. "Not at all."

"It is good of you to overlook my lapse."

"No problem," Thomas murmured.

"Yeah, don't even worry about it."

Thomas was trying not to gape, or leer, and Fred actually had a bit of sympathy for the guy. He'd been minding his own business in his underwater dorm room, and suddenly two naked women were dripping all over his tile.

In fact, Thomas was so determinedly making eye contact and avoiding looking elsewhere, his own eyes were almost watering. Given that Tennian was lithe, exotic, and pretty, and had the nicest set of knockers Fred had ever seen outside of a Victoria's Secret catalog, that was quite an accomplishment.

"I saw you outside," he said, then coughed to clear his throat. When he continued, he sounded more like a man and less like a Ford 4×4. "You were like—like a daydream I had once."

Tennian smiled shyly, and Fred was startled—and annoyed—to feel a stab of jealousy. And not a little poke, either, but a vicious stab. It felt like someone had slammed an icicle through her chest. Her face was probably as green as her hair right now.

Jealousy?

Not only was it stupid, it was pointless. She had absolutely no right to that emotion at all. She'd spent an awful lot of time shoving Thomas *and* Artur away. And had been devastated when they'd both actually up and left. Now here they were, the three of them, together again. And she was still pushing them away.

Make up your damned mind, she told herself savagely, *very* glad she wasn't underwater where just anyone could pick up her thoughts.

Pick one, or pick neither, or become a Mormon and pick both, but stop all this wishy-washy *bullshit*.

"—known Fredrika for long?"

"We met a year ago. Your king sent Artur to Boston—that's a city on the coast—"

"She lives in Chesapeake Bay, Thomas," Fred said, exasperated.

"Oh. Then you know where Boston is. Anyway, King Mekkam sent Artur to find Fred and help figure out who was dumping poison into the bay."

"Yes, yes!" Tennian actually jumped up and down. This did excellent things to her cleavage. Thomas's eyes watered even more. "His Highness Prince Artur had many exciting tales when he returned! We were shocked that he took life, but it seems as though the villain left him no choice."

"Not hardly. He was shooting up the place. He shot Fred, too."

"Yes! It was so exciting!" Tennian glanced at Fred. "Ah, although it was regrettable that you were injured."

"Oh, she was totally fine," Thomas said, waving away Fred's gunshot wound to the chest. She glared at him so hard she thought her skull was going to crack, but he was oblivious. "But anyway, here you are, so let me show you around. This is the galley—are you hungry? Do you want a snack?"

"She had one outside," Fred said, still shuddering at the memory. She wondered if Thomas would still be so infatuated once he saw gentle, shy Tennian chow her way through the belly of a nurse shark. "She's probably still got fish scales in her teeth."

"Great, that's great. Something to drink?"

"Your tiny house makes drinks?"

"Sure!" Thomas opened the small, silver fridge. "Here, have a Coke. Do you like Coke?"

Tennian found she did. In fact, the caffeine and sugar from the three Cokes made her as talkative as she ever got out of water. In fact, for Tennian, she was practically gushing.

"—so shiny and beautiful from the outside! I was drawn to it like—like—"

"A crow is drawn to tinfoil?" Fred suggested.

Thomas gave her a look. "Never mind Dr. Sourpuss over there; she's always grouchy. And here's where I sleep."

Fred had been following them through the small ship,

feeling out of place but also strangely reluctant to leave the two of them alone. Thomas was a mermaid geek; when he was a little boy his mom had read him all kinds of mermaid stories and the lonely little boy (his dad was always off on some mystery job or other) often fantasized about finding a friend in the sea. He'd become a marine biologist as a direct result of those stories, and that childhood.

And maybe . . . maybe he only liked Fred *because* she was a mermaid. To posit that further, maybe he'd like *any* mermaid.

Well, sure he would. And why not? God knew Fred was no Miss Congeniality. She wasn't even a Miss October. And this month Thomas was going to meet scads of mermaids. Hundreds. Maybe even thousands.

Her rotten luck that he ran into Tennian, who was apparently pretty open-minded for her people. Any other mermaid probably would have been scared shitless of him (treacherous bipeds, don't you know). Or disdainful. But not this mermaid. Of all the rotten! Damned! Luck!

Tennian was patting the bed, then sitting on it, then bouncing on it. "If you can't sleep underwater and let the current rock you, this is likely the next best thing," she said, her blue hair flying all over the place as she bounced, bounced, bounced. Thomas lost the battle and stared at her breasts, which were also bouncing.

"So. I. Uh." Thomas cleared his throat. "I noticed you're a natural—I mean, that's your natural hair color. I mean, obviously it's your natural hair color. A very, um, striking and vivid blue. Is that, um, common in your family? Ow!"

"I'm sorry," Fred said sweetly. "Was that your kneecap?"

"Right, thanks," he muttered. Then, louder, "Sorry, Tennian, those were pretty rude questions. It's not every day I have a naked, gorgeous mermaid in my—ow, goddammit!"

"I'm sorry. Was that your other kneecap?"

Thomas hobbled over to the chair in the corner and sat down, groaning softly.

"Are you well, Thomas?" Tennian asked, stopping in mid-bounce.

"As well as can be expected," he said through gritted teeth, rubbing his knees. "Anyway, that's all of the URV."

"It is wonderful!"

"Thank you. I worked hard on it."

"What, work?" Fred scoffed. "You drew up the plans and then hired a bunch of people to build it for you."

"You know how many sex scenes I had to write to afford this thing?" Thomas griped. "Let's just say all my characters aren't going to be doing anything below the shoulders for a while. I'm so burned out it's not even funny."

"Burned out? Sex scenes?"

"Biped talk," Thomas said hastily.

"Don't you want to tell Tennian about your girlie books?"

"Maybe later. Say, Tennian, do you know when the Pelagic is supposed to start?"

"Tomorrow morning. His Majesty wanted to give you and Fredrika plenty of time to rest from your travels."

"Well, that was thoughtful. Oh, that reminds me, Mekkam's coming back tonight for season three. I don't know when the guy sleeps."

"Season three?" Fred yelped. "You couldn't have tried him out on the Discovery Channel? Let him watch *Meerkat Manor* or a show about grubs? Jeez, anything but HBO, even *Dirty Jobs*, fer Crissakes."

"Look, he saw me watching *Deadwood*, he wanted to watch *Deadwood*. I'm supposed to tell a king what to do? Back off, Fred, or I'll put the bullet I pulled out of you right back in."

"I'd like to see you try, Romance Boy. I can't believe that out of all the people the king could be hanging out with, he picked you."

"That will be very helpful for you," Tennian said, shaking the last can of Coke in a vain attempt to get three or four more drops out. "Do you know why?"

"Uh . . ."

Fred made an impatient sound. "Because when the rest of her people find out Mekkam likes you enough to hang out in the URV and watch HBO reruns, they'll warm up to you a lot quicker than they normally would have."

"Oh." Thomas looked surprised, then pleased. "I didn't think of it like that. You don't suppose Mekkam's faking the interest, is he?"

"Our king does not *fake*," Tennian said, all trace of mirth gone from her face. She had been rolling around in the blankets but now abruptly sat up.

"Okay, sorry. I didn't mean to offend, or imply that

King Mekkam lied. It's just hard for Fred and me to accept all this in such a short time. She's a half-and-half, and I'm a surface dweller, but the royal family is welcoming us with open arms. You can't blame us for wondering."

"I can, but I shall not." Tennian shook her head and looked wry. "Only bipeds would view the gift of friendship with suspicion."

"Yeah, sneaky rotten bipeds like Thomas, here," Fred said helpfully. "Disgusting! Two hairy legs, no tail, no stamina in the open water . . . It's enough to make you barf, when you think about it!"

"It's probably just the novelty. Which in Fred's case, at least, wears off," Thomas joked.

At least, she was pretty sure he was joking.

Fred resisted the urge to kick him in the knee again. One to grow on, as her stepfather might have said.

Nineteen

"And then . . . then! He was practically slobbering all over her. Granted, she was a gorgeous naked woman with striking blue hair—and blue pubic hair—but still."

"Fred."

"Slobbering! Like a summer hound." Fred was pacing back and forth beside the pool. "And she was all, 'Oh, Thomas, you're so clever. Oh, Thomas, you built such a pretty underwater dorm room. Oh, Thomas, can I have a tenth Coke?' Sickening."

"Fred."

She stopped pacing and stood over him. "And why do I even care, anyway? Don't I have enough to worry about without giving a crap if Thomas likes a mermaid who isn't me?"

"Fred!"

"What?" she snapped.

"Move." Jonas, clad in crimson swim trunks patterned with green sea horses, and sunglasses (which he'd picked up at the small gift shop off the kitchen), and nothing else, shaded his eyes with a forearm and squinted up at her. "You're standing in my light. Then I'll have a Fred-shaped shadow across my rock-hard abs, and Barb will laugh at me so much I'll lose my hard-on."

"Gross!" she squealed.

"Hey, it's reality, baby. Deal. And speaking of reality, were you planning on hiding Thomas from all the other mermaids?"

"No."

"And you're not in love with him, or Artur. In fact, it sort of pisses you off when they start—how'd you put it? Slobbering? It's no secret that you get mad when they slobber all over you."

"I know, I know! I'm aware of how stupid and junior high all of this is."

"Well, get your shit together," her alleged best friend said heartlessly. "Either you want Thomas (or Artur), or you don't want Thomas (or Artur). Pick one. Or don't. But shouldn't you be worrying more about the Pelagic than about the sad, pathetic state of your love life? Your love life is always pathetic, but Pelagics only come along once every three or four decades."

Fred plunked down on the concrete beside her best friend. Funny how Jonas's sensible advice often sounded like the advice she gave herself. In fact, sometimes the advice she gave herself actually sounded like Jonas.

"Yeah, everything you're saying is a hundred percent right. But I'm not a computer, Jonas. I can't turn it off like a switch."

"At last, she admits she has feelings!" He adjusted his sunglasses. "A breakthrough."

"Shut up."

"So what'd you end up doing?"

"Oh, Tennian offered to show him the Cayman Trench."

Jonas snickered.

"Don't be such a pig. It's not a sexual euphemism."

"Are you sure?"

She ignored that. "He'll need scuba gear, but she'll give him an all-expense-paid mermaid tour."

"And of course he took her up on it."

"Of course!" Fred had to admit, even to herself, that Thomas could not be faulted for that, no matter how hard she tried. "He's a mermaid geek, remember. He would have taken Artur or Kertal up on it, too. Not that Kertal would have asked. But— Oh, shit! That reminds me. My dad was a traitor."

"Yeah, I heard."

She nearly fell into the pool. "What?"

Jonas adjusted his sunglasses. "Artur told me. He was worried some of the other mer-dudes might give you shit. I said you wouldn't give a shit if they gave you shit. He seemed relieved about you not giving a shit about getting shit, and then he dropped the whole thing."

"Swell. Why didn't you tell me?"

"He asked me not to. He was trying to figure out how to break it to you."

"And you agreed to this?"

Jonas yawned, unmoved by her wrath. "Hey, calm

down. I gave him until the end of the week. If he hadn't spilled it to you by then, I would have."

"Neither of you did. Tennian gave me the whole story. And after Daddy-o's little takeover failed, they kicked him out."

"Huh." Jonas sat up, examined his (not very tan) stomach, then lay back down. "I didn't get that part of the story."

"And then he washed up onshore and knocked up my mom."

"What a lovely ending to a depressing story."

"Which reminds me—"

"—we aren't telling Moon that your dad was the bad guy a generation ago. Got it."

Fred almost smiled. It was so comforting, being around someone who knew her so well.

"Maybe you should go tell Thomas you want to fuck."

"What?"

"Date! I meant date."

"Yeah, but . . ." She had tried to picture herself doing just that. And had frozen like a Mrs. Paul's fish stick every time. Nor could she picture herself telling Artur the same thing.

She wasn't afraid of them. Not afraid they'd hurt her, at least. She wasn't afraid of any man. And she liked sex (if memory served). But the thought of essentially telling one person, *one* man, "I'm going to make myself vulnerable to you, so hurt at will!" was terrifying. Her throat actually went dry when she contemplated it.

"You're such a chickenshit," Jonas said kindly, accurately reading her expression. "Would it kill you to *try* being in a relationship?"

"Says the guy who got dumped about a thousand times before hooking up with my boss."

"Yeah, and it was all worth it to find Barb, ya idjit!"

Fred said nothing. It would be too cruel (even for her) to remind Jonas of all the times he'd sobbed into his couch. The times he'd ignored his personal grooming for as long as a week when he'd been dumped. The way he'd eat trans fats to get over a breakup. Or wear socks that didn't match his tie.

She shuddered, recalling the horror.

Oh, sure, Dr. Barb was in his life now and everything was rosy. Oh, yes, everything was swell, including his view of all past breakups.

No, she wouldn't remind him of the pain he so

conveniently glossed over. Nor was she in a hurry to go through anything like that on her own.

She had the nagging thought that she was being a coward, and shoved it right back out of her brain.

"Meanwhile," her friend was nagging, "you've got two awesome guys who would chew off their own arms—or each other's—for the chance to make you happy, and all you can do is freak out."

"Yup." Fred glumly rested her chin in her hand. "Freaking out. That's all I can do. It's all I've *been* doing ever since I got here. And the damn Pelagic hasn't even started yet!"

"Well, worry about that, then. And if Tennian gets fresh with Thomas, sock her."

She grinned down at her friend. "Now *that's* advice I can use."

Twenty

§

To her extreme annoyance, Jonas's mouth fell open and he stared past her as she bitched about the URV, Thomas, Tennian, the Pelagic, her mom, and her period, which was due within the week.

"Oh my God, help me remember my hot girlfriend," her friend murmured, and Fred knew without turning around that it was—

"Good evening, Fredrika. Sir. I thought I might—if you did not mind, I thought I might . . . dine . . . with you?"

"Tennian, Jonas. Jonas, you remember Tennian."

Tennian the hottie, who has apparently started following me around. "Sure. We'd love it if you had supper with us."

Jonas had bounded to his feet and was shaking hands with the nudely gleaming Tennian. "Hi there! Niceta see you again! Chilly this time of night, eh?"

"It is good to see you, sir. I have heard many nice things about you."

"You have?" Jonas was frankly staring. "About me? Not from her, anyway." Jerking a thumb in Fred's direction.

"You'd better drop it while you can still count to five on that hand," she muttered. Then, louder: "Nice to see you again."

"Indeed!" Tennian glanced down at herself, then back up. "Fredrika, may I impose upon you? I require clothing."

"Sure, sure, there's plenty in my hut."

"Nonsense!" boomed her friend (who, laughably, was thought to be gay by the casual bystander). "It's a come-as-you-are dinner! No need for shorts. Or a shirt!"

Tennian smiled at him. "You are kind, but I will abide by your customs."

"Nuts."

Without another word, Fred led Tennian toward her hut.

Tennian was devouring meat loaf (What, Fred wondered, could it be made of? Were there cows on the island?) and listening to the others chatter. Even Fred, slightly begrudging the lovely girl's company, couldn't deny that Tennian was fascinated and thrilled to be taking a meal with them. It was kind of fun to be ringside.

"—of course I came down like a shot. The prince was really great to invite me," Thomas was saying, his plate untouched in front of him.

Fred rudely stuck her finger in his mashed potatoes, then sucked on her finger. He noticed, but didn't care . . . just pushed his plate closer to her.

She hated mashed potatoes.

"You give me too much honor," Artur replied amiably, gulping down a fourth helping of conch chowder. "My good father invited you. I only extended the invitation on his behalf."

"Aw, come on, you're being too modest."

"Not very damn likely," Fred muttered to her corn chowder.

129

"We're breaking ground, right here." Thomas gestured to the room, still creepily decorated with nets and baby dolls. And to the diners: himself, Artur, Jonas, Fred, Tennian. "Surface dwellers and Undersea Folk getting along fine. Shit, Fred and Jonas are best friends! I think this is really promising for how the Pelagic will turn out. And for future relations with our people, of course."

"Apples and oranges," Fred muttered.

"And Fred is a hybrid," Artur said, nicely but with no doubt about his meaning. "Who did not know her people until recently. Who else did she have to befriend but Jonas? No offense, good sir," he added hastily.

"Hey, none taken," Jonas said, working on his third Bloody Mary. "It was either me or Sandy Caturia, and Sandy was a nose picker."

Fred was startled into a snicker; she hadn't thought of their nose-mining fellow student in many years. "Don't sell yourself short, jerk. You've been a good friend."

"Yeah, but that's not the issue, is it?" Thomas asked intently. "It's not who Fred picked to be her friend, it's who decided to befriend her. And even if she was buds with the president of the United States, the fact that she's a hybrid would always bring doubt on that friendship, right?"

Artur looked uncomfortable, but could not lie. Not that Fred gave a shit, but it was interesting to watch him wiggle. "You speak the truth, Thomas; it is one of your finest qualities, and also the most exasperating. Although I daresay Fred could befriend anyone she wished."

"Sure, she's a regular Miss Congeniality," Jonas snickered.

"I have heard horror stories about surface dwellers for nearly all my fifty years," Tennian commented, pausing for a minute to suck the meat out of a tiny lobster leg, then chew up said tiny leg, "but I had never known one well enough to talk to. You do not seem like barbarians to me."

Fred jabbed an elbow into Thomas's side. "Fifty. Didja hear that? *Fifty!* Hope you packed the URV with Depends."

"I think it's like anything else," Jonas said, getting up to fix himself another Bloody Mary. "With every species. Some of 'em are assholes, some of 'em are saints, but most fall somewhere in between."

"O my Tennian," Artur said, smiling, "you will have your nose everywhere, will you not? So it has been," he told the others, "since we were children together."

"Your Highness implies equality among our families

when there is none. You lead, we follow. That is the way of it."

Hmm, Fred hmm'd. Tennian was being too modest. She came from important people; that was obvious. Maybe the Undersea Folk equivalent of aristocrats?

"In this, you are leading, and it pleases me greatly," Artur said.

Tennian didn't blush, but she stared into her glass and said nothing. Fred figured Artur meant the huge step of walking out of the ocean and taking a meal with Traitor Bait.

"His Highness knows of my stubborn streak."

"His Highness," Artur said, creepily referring to himself in the third person, "has had cause to be grateful for it more than once."

The two Undersea Folk shared a warm look which Fred, later by her own admission, would admit she completely misread.

So she slid over until she and Artur were hip to hip, climbed onto his lap, and planted a kiss on his mouth (which was hanging open with surprise).

Twenty-one

🌊

"Whuf?" Artur managed, or something close to it. But Fred was lost in the sea of sensation she had brought upon herself. She could feel her thighs warming against Artur's (darned cutoffs); could feel his warm mouth recover from the surprise and begin actively kissing her back; could feel his ridiculously strong arms wrap around her.

She kissed him, she kissed him, she kissed him and forgot about the Pelagic, and her father, and the way Tennian had apparently bewitched both of the men Fred refused to date. She even, for a brief glorious moment, forgot about Moon, Jonas, and Dr. Barb.

"Say, is that the time?" Jonas exclaimed, speak of the devil. "It's so late, it's, uh, way past my bedtime. Way way way past."

"It's seven twenty-five," Thomas said, sounding (hooray! Wait, what?) disgruntled.

"Right, that's what I meant. Time to call Fred's boss and get me some phone sex."

"Is this, ah, I don't mean to intrude on a cultural taboo," Tennian said, "but is this normal for—"

"Fred? No. Ordinary people surrounded by hotties? Yes. Come on, gorgeous. I'm dying to fix your hair."

"It does not need fixing," Tennian commented, and, thank goodness, her voice was getting fainter.

"Oh, honey! The things you don't know, living like a slug on the bottom of the sea. First we'll do a protein pack. Then a trim, I think. How about a crew cut? Your bone structure would be killer with that look."

The door shut and, with sweet suddenness, Fred and Artur were alone.

She stopped kissing him at once.

"Ah, my Rika, I think you have left this tiny portion of my mouth unexplored." Her legs dangled as he pointed to a minuscule spot on his lower lip. "Perhaps you should see to it at once."

"Don't get any funny ideas," she warned him, looking around. Yep, Jonas and Tennian were gone. So was Thomas, although she hadn't heard him leave. The guy could move like a cat when he wanted. "I was just—just—"

"Marking your territory, as do your dogs?" the prince teased, shifting her weight on his lap so she rested easier. "I have no objection to being marked, Little Rika. Not by one such as you."

"She has a lot of nerve, don't you think?" Fred cried, beating her fists on Artur's chest. "First she bewitches Thomas, then she throws herself at you. There's only so much a girl can take, even one with a (sometimes) tail."

Artur stared at her for a moment, then threw back his head and did the kingly booming laugh thing. "Tennian! And I! Oh no, oh no, oh no-no-no."

He tapered off into snorts and giggles, but when she tried to climb out of his lap he tightened his grip and she stopped. "Don't even say it."

"I do not have to, Little Rika, you have deduced it on your own."

"Tennian wasn't making a play for you."

"We are cousins," he explained gently, but his red eyes gleamed and gleamed until they looked like lamps. "We played together as babies."

"Oh, friggin' great!" Fred threw up her hands and nearly dislodged herself from Artur's lap. "Cousins! Which nobody bothered to tell me! Doesn't that make her an earl or a duchess or something?"

"Tennian's family has always eschewed titles," he explained, stroking her waist with both hands. "She did not knowingly deceive you."

"She doesn't knowingly irritate the shit out of me, either, but guess what?"

"That is not what I would deem an exclusive club, Little Rika."

"Hmph." Fred slumped, sulked, crossed her arms over her chest, kicked her feet. "I guess it's not such a big deal, then."

"Ah, but it is, Little Rika. I like your jealousy. In fact, I adore it greatly."

"I wasn't jealous," she lied. "Just showing her she's not the only hottie at the table."

"Very wise," he said gravely, "but even now I am having inappropriate thoughts about my father's brother's daughter. Perhaps you should remind me of your hottie status."

"You wish," she began, but his lips covered hers and that was as far as she got.

Twenty-two

$\mathfrak{z}$

Fred spent another sleepless night fantasizing about surgically removing Tennian's ears and then stuffing them in her mouth.

And wondering if she had "bad" blood . . . traitor's blood.

And wishing King Mekkam wasn't quite so infatuated with the *Deadwood* prostitutes. (Apparently the queen, Artur's mother, was long dead.)

And wondering if she shied away from committing to

either of the men in her life because of honest disinterest, or fear.

It hadn't been easy, extricating herself from Artur's lap and grasp. Not least because she had been *way* too tempted to remain. But after a few well-placed kicks she'd been free to go . . . though if she'd known she was going to be in for a night of staring at the ceiling, she might have lingered.

The alarm went off—not that it woke her—and she was glad. Anything was better than lying in bed fretting.

And it was all so stupid! It's not like she'd been hurt in other relationships, she thought, throwing the blankets back and beginning to get dressed. In fact, far from it.

Her adult life had been a series of one or two dates, blind dates, and occasional work dates. She hadn't been interested in boys as a high school student, and then she'd been so busy at UMass there hadn't been time for a steady relationship. And then she'd been concentrating on getting her Ph.D., and then her work at the aquarium had pretty much consumed her time.

She'd just never had *time* for a serious relationship. It had nothing at all to do with keeping men at a distance so they couldn't reject her as a freak of nature.

Wait. Where had *that* come from?

Then she realized what she was doing, cursed, and pulled off all the clothes she'd just carefully put on. She couldn't wear *clothes* to the Pelagic, for God's sake! Nobody else would, that was for sure. She'd stand out enough without showing up in shorts and a shirt.

Naked, she walked out the door and nearly ran Jonas over.

"Whoa! Where's the fire? My goodness, you're looking . . . perky."

"Shut up," she growled.

Jonas fell into step beside her as she walked toward the surf. "Don't take this the wrong way, but you look hideous. You're hardly even pretty this morning."

"Didn't sleep."

"Who could, with all that pressure you're under? Look, don't worry about it, they'll love you."

Fred snorted.

"Right, okay, well, they'll think you're interesting at the very least."

"Do I keep men at a distance because I'm afraid they'll reject me once they know I can grow scales?"

"Yes. Now just remember to be yourself. And—"

She skidded to a halt in the sand. "Wait. Yes?"

"Sure. Don't you remember Jeff Dawson asking you out in our sophomore year? And Mark Dalton our junior year? And—"

"Those were all varsity morons."

"Yeah, but you could have gone out if you'd wanted. You just didn't want to." She'd started walking again, and he was hurrying to keep pace. "Now don't let the other mermaids intimidate you. And play nice with the other kids. And—"

"Be myself? That's your advice? Be grouchy and antisocial and foulmouthed?"

"And it wouldn't hurt you to say please and thank you once in a while."

"Thanks for all the swell advice, Jonas." She plowed into the surf, thankful once again that the water was so pleasant. "Don't wait up."

"And try not to pick any fights! It's bad for your complexion!" he yelled after her, and then she was diving beneath the waves into that other world, her father's world, and, mercifully, Jonas was very effectively cut off.

Twenty-three

She forgot all of Jonas's advice the minute she saw Tennian's twin.

Good morning, she thought at him.

He was talking to two mermaids and a merman—the merman was Kertal, but she didn't recognize the women—and didn't turn.

GOOD MORNING, JACKASS! Then she swam right up behind him and poked him rudely between the shoulder blades.

She thought she saw Kertal grin, but couldn't be sure.

Tennian's brother slowly turned around and said, with great reluctance, *Good morning.*

I'm Fred. And you are . . . ?

Rennan.

Hello again, Fredrika, Kertal said politely. He gestured to the women, one a tiny creature with true black hair—not dark brown, *black*—and matching eyes, the other long and slender, with grenadine-colored hair and eyes. *This is Meerna, and Bettan.*

Hi, ladies.

It was kind of you to join us, Kertal added.

Oh, heck, I wouldn't have missed it. So! Isn't it so incredibly awkward that my father tried to overthrow the monarchy three decades ago?

Again, she thought she saw a smile on Kertal's face, but it vanished too quickly for her to be sure.

The small, black-haired mermaid blinked and finally replied, *Yes. I suppose that is awkward.*

Is it true you've lived nearly all your life on the surface? the tall redhead asked. She was pale, like every Undersea Folk Fred had ever met, but so pale her skin was almost translucent. She'd probably burst into flames if she ever set foot on land.

Yeah, that's true. I never knew my father, so I never knew about you guys.

Then it is well that King Mekkam found you.

Fred wasn't sure about that at all, but now wasn't the time. *I s'pose.*

I need to see to my sister, Rennan said stiffly. *Excuse me.*

Super great to see you again! Fred thought after him. *Let's have lunch!*

I do not think he will dine with you, Kertal said soberly.

No shit. I was just yanking his chain. I can handle anything but being ignored.

And in that, Bettan said coolly, *you are much like your sire.*

Without another word, she swam off.

Oh, Jonas, Fred thought, suddenly terribly lonesome for her friend, for land, for the sky, for *air. What good is being myself if they've already made up their minds about me?*

Well. We had better go take our places, Kertal said. *It was—it was nice to see you again.*

Good-bye, Meerna added, not looking Fred in the eye. And off they swam.

Fred slowly swam after them, taking her time so they could pull as far ahead of her as they liked. She could see several clusters of Undersea Folk, and simply followed them.

A few miles out from shore, they were plenty deep but it was difficult to swim anywhere without bumping into a mermaid. She caught herself looking for spotlights or bleachers and reminded herself that this was not going to be like any other meeting she had attended. Why in the world was she picturing an underwater pep rally?

For one thing, even if a boom mike could somehow work down here, it wouldn't be needed in a group of telepaths. Which reminded her, Thomas was going to have no idea what they were talking about.

Hmm. Perhaps the king wasn't being quite as openminded as they were giving him credit for. What did he care if a surface dweller who already knew about mermaids saw a bunch of them getting together? Especially when the only way he'd know what they were discussing would be if someone told him?

And, speak of the devil, here came the URV, gliding almost silently toward her. She could see Thomas behind one of the windows, at the controls, and he waved madly at her before settling down to navigate. The URV glided past her and then settled into what appeared to be a stationary orbit, giving Thomas several angles to shoot from.

And, as with any school of fish, there were a lot more Undersea Folk than appeared at first glance. She tried to estimate and thought there were at least five hundred that she could see. And the meeting would be "projected" telepathically to the Undersea Folk who wished to participate but couldn't make it to the Caymans in time.

Unbelievable.

Most of them were slender, with the typically longer tail that was broader at the hips. The tails were all in shades of blue or green (or both), while hair and eye color tended to match, or only be off by a shade. Attending the Pelagic was like looking at a fabulous living rainbow, because there were no brunettes or blonds or strawberry blonds. No, there were blue-haired folk, orange-haired, forest green, cotton candy pink, buttercup yellow . . .

Unbelievable.

And there was apparently some sort of statute that all Undersea Folk had to be attractive, because they all *were*. It was ridiculous.

(It did not occur to Fred that she wasn't exactly hard to look at, either.)

She was staring, and knew it, and was helpless to stop. But that was all right, because she caught quite a few people looking at her as well.

Looking at her, and then looking at each other. Talking to each other. Gossiping, to be perfectly blunt. But Fred couldn't hear them. So perhaps Undersea Folk telepathy was a little more complicated than she had first imagined. You couldn't "overhear" something you weren't meant to; the thought had to be projected at you, into your mind.

She thought, *Too bad about all those great whites headed this way.* But it was just a stray thought; she wasn't trying to "talk" to anyone, or be overheard.

Nobody looked toward her; nobody reacted.

Hmmm.

Let the Pelagic come to order, Mekkam's voice boomed in her head, and just like that, it had begun.

Twenty-four

Fred paid careful attention, but found she was able to eyeball the other Undersea Folk while following the events of the Pelagic, and that was fine by her.

And she was beginning to get an idea why her father had wanted to overthrow King Mekkam. How had Tennian explained it? An accident of birth? Mekkam's mind-touch?

Well, that was for sure; Mekkam controlled the meeting and kept everyone on track, *and* made sure Undersea Folk halfway around the world could "hear" what was going on as well. No friggin' wonder he was the king! And if Artur had that kind of telepathy, it was no shock that he'd be the king after Mekkam bit the big one.

How, Fred wondered, *could my dad have ever thought he could overthrow this guy?* For one thing, Mekkam could *read everybody's mind.* Even if, as she suspected, an Undersea Folk had to make an effort, put a specific thought into somebody's mind, Mekkam could still probably head off any plot he wanted.

She shook off thoughts of her traitorous (and apparently idiotic) father and focused on the Pelagic.

The way Mekkam explained it to everyone (though she imagined most of the people at the Pelagic knew the scoop), there were two basic factions among the Undersea Folk.

The Air Breathers, mostly younger Folk who didn't necessarily think the king was the be-all and end-all, felt that hiding from the surface dwellers was something out of the twentieth century (and the nineteenth, and the eighteenth . . .).

The Air Breathers felt they had just as much right to walk around on land as any surface dweller and they didn't want to spend even one more generation in hiding.

The Traditionals, those who follow the dictates of the royal family without question, felt that the royal family has had it right for the past six generations: there is far, far more ocean than land, and there was more than enough to hide from bipeds while at the same time living a comfortable life.

Thus, the Pelagic: a meeting to decide whether the Undersea Folk were going to stay hidden . . . or show themselves to CNN, among others.

Once Fred realized exactly what was at stake, she began to get a niggling feeling about the reason why she had been urged to attend. Because she, unlike anyone else here, was a child of both worlds. She imagined it was only a matter of time before Mekkam called for her testimony.

And what in the world would she say?

Twenty-five

Then what happened?

Fred accepted a Coke—she was amazed Tennian had left any in the URV's galley—and cracked the can open, then slurped up the foam before any could hit her shirt. Well, Thomas's shirt. He had offered her a clean pair of boxers and one of his T-shirts, and her hair was bound up in a towel. At least she wasn't parading around naked in front of him. Anymore. For today.

It was different when she was in her tail form, that

was all. It could be argued she was just as naked then, but it sure felt different.

"Fred? Then what happened?"

"Oh. Sorry." She forced herself to quit contemplating Thomas's boxer shorts and answered him. "Then a bunch of my dad's people got up and reminded everyone—like we needed it—that you horrible surface dwellers are treacherous, disgusting, rotten sonsabitches who shit where you eat."

Thomas raised an eyebrow at her, and she shrugged in return. "Don't forget, you were the only biped Artur had ever met who *didn't* shit where he ate."

"Yeah, yeah, don't remind me. So that's really what all this is about? It's just that some of the mermaids really want to come out of the closet?"

"Yep, some of them do. They just have to talk all the others into it. And don't belittle it; it's a huge deal."

"So they're going to, what? Debate back and forth?"

"Until Mekkam figures out a majority are ready to vote. Then they'll—we'll—vote."

Thomas perched on the tiny galley counter. "I guess it has to be all or nothing, doesn't it? If fifty of them want to walk up on a beach, they can't unless the entire—what?

Race? Species? Anyway, they all have to be on the same side, don't they?"

"Yeah, they—"

"So how are you going to vote?"

"Me?" she gasped. "I'm still freaking out over being invited; I have no idea how I'll vote."

"Vote yes!" Thomas begged. He leapt off the counter, seized her by the hands, and began to waltz her around the tiny galley. "Then we won't have to hide your tail from all my cousins. We can get married at the New England Aquarium and go swimming in Main One."

"Let me go!" she protested, trying not to giggle at the thought of her in the main tank, clad in her tail and a bridal veil. "Stop acting like such a numskull."

He dipped her. "Marry me, vote yes, come out of the water closet—get it?—and we'll see the world in the URV."

"Will you stop goofing around?" She struggled out of the dip and (gently) removed his hands from her. He was just clowning around; Jonas did the same thing every damned day.

Except her heart didn't pound when Jonas did it. She didn't feel faint when Jonas did it. She—

The intercom buzzed and Thomas hopped down from the counter. "That's Jonas."

"Agh!"

He raised an eyebrow at her. "Uh, sorry, I didn't think it would, y'know, terrify you. Having him here and all. I called him when it looked like you guys were breaking it off for the day. Hit the red button and then come on in!" he called.

Fred swallowed her disappointment. She had hoped to have a bit more alone time with Thomas. After spending the day surrounded by her father's kind, and with various people in her head of all places, she was hoping to wind down with one, count 'em, *one* fella. And not Jonas, though she loved him to death.

"My Christ, that's a long swim!" Jonas gasped. "I felt like Flipper's stunt double!" He was dripping wet (naturally), his snorkel and mask dangling from one hand. Unlike most of the people who walked through the air lock, he was wearing shorts and fins. He stood on one foot to yank each flipper off. "You'll be sorry if I drown on the way out here."

"I'm moored not even fifty yards offshore," Thomas protested mildly. "There's almost no tidal activity to swim against and the water's crystal clear all the way out. Admit it: you're only on the Islands to work on your tan."

"I'd never deny that," Jonas said, tossing the fins in a corner and then hopping up and down on one foot, shaking his head. "I swear to God, I've got half a gallon of water in each ear."

"Is that why you swam out here?" Fred asked, taking another gulp of Coke. "To bitch?"

"Naw. So tell me about the big meeting."

Briefly, Fred filled him in on day one of the Pelagic.

"Huh. Well, that explains why they were so hot to get you down here," Jonas said.

"It's a really good thing," Thomas commented, "that you're smarter than you look."

"Fuck off, Pearson, or I'll never buy another one of your sleazy books ever again. So how are you going to plead?"

"What?" Fred asked.

"For or against humanity?"

"I don't know," she admitted. "I haven't had a lot of time to think about it."

"I think you should tell 'em to go for it. I think the

Air Breather contingent has a point: Why *should* they hide from most of the planet? It's just as much theirs as it is ours."

"I don't know," Thomas said quietly. "As a species, we've got a long history of intolerance and genocide. Maybe they're better off staying hidden. The oceans are gigantic. We'd never have to know. Hell, they managed to convince all of *us* that they're myths. That's quite a trick, when you think of it. A shame to undo it."

"See, that's where I run into problems." Fred finished her Coke. "I can see both sides of the issue. There're plenty of reasons to do it. There're plenty not to, also."

"Is that what you're going to get up there and say? 'Hi, my name is Fred, my dad tried to kill the royal family and I'm not sure if you should speak up or stay hidden.' Hmm, that actually might make Artur fall out of love with you." Jonas began excitedly jumping around the URV. "That could do the trick!"

"Shut up, Jonas. You're supposed to be helping."

"I am helping," he said, hurt.

"You want to make Artur fall out of love with you?" Thomas asked, leaning forward.

"I'm just—we're just joking around."

"Because," he added, giving her a slow grin, "I know a perfect way to do that. Or, if not make him fall out of love, at least really make him mad."

"Down, boy." But Fred couldn't help it; she grinned back.

Twenty-six

§

The intercom beeped again. They could hear the air
lock re-cycling, and then the king of the Undersea Folk
stepped inside. "Hello, my motherfuckers," he said cheerfully.

Fred smacked her forehead and simultaneously glared
at Thomas, who was laughing like a hyena.

"Sorry, *what* did you say?" Jonas gasped.

"Are you letting these other motherfuckers know
what went on in the Pelagic?"

"Yeah, and after that we're going to hunt up some

whores and pan for gold." She whirled on Thomas.
"You couldn't have shown him an Animal Planet DVD,
ohhh, noooo."

Thomas shrugged. "What can I say? King Mekkam
likes what he likes."

"I did not mean to interrupt your motherfucking
meeting," Mekkam went on, far too perkily given the
long day they'd all had.

He was in pretty good shape for someone who was
close to a hundred years old. His chest was broad, and
grizzled with graying red hair. His shoulder-length hair
was also streaked with gray, but he wasn't "in good
shape for his age." He was in good shape, period.

"But I wanted to warn you, you little motherfucker,
that I will be calling on your testimony first thing tomorrow. Also, my motherfucking son is on the way to your
hut to ask you to dine."

"Great," Thomas muttered. "Uh, guys, the URV wasn't
exactly built to hold all of us at once."

"I can take a motherfucking hint, Thomas."

"So can I," Jonas said, still giving Mekkam incredu-
lous glances.

"I thought you were trying to make Artur fall out of

love with you," Thomas added, and was he—was that a sulk?

"The last thing I should be worrying about right now is my love life," she informed him, but why was his unhappiness making her so darned happy? It was sick, that was all, sick, *sick*!

"I don't suppose . . ." Mekkam began hopefully.

"Sir, that's it. There aren't any more. They cancelled the series," Thomas explained.

"Cold-blooded bastard motherfuckers."

"Yes, that's exactly what the Bring Back *Deadwood* chat rooms were buzzing about. Too bad. Well, goodbye."

"You have no more cultural documents I can view?"

"No!" Fred and Jonas shouted in unison.

Thomas folded like origami. "Well . . . I could probably find something . . ."

"I'm outta here," Fred muttered. "Where's Artur?"

Mekkam's gaze went faraway and after a long moment he said, "He is coming ashore now, intent on knocking on the door of your hut."

"You—you know that? You can find him with your mind?" Thomas asked, fascinated.

"Of course." Mekkam actually shrugged. "That is what it means to be king."

"Any of them?" Thomas was nearly stammering in his excitement. "You can find any of the Undersea Folk? Anytime you like?"

"Of course."

"Is that how you found me?" Fred asked quietly.

"Yes, Fredrika. But I felt it prudent to leave you with your mother until—"

"Until you needed me," she finished bitterly.

"Until you were ready to meet your father's people," he said, correcting her with firm gentleness.

"Oh." She swallowed. "Uh. Sorry."

"Quite all right, my little motherfucker."

"That's *it*." Fred's hand slammed down on the air lock release. "I'm outta here."

"Wait, wait!" Jonas cried. "Uh, Mekkam—king, sir, whatever—one thing I don't get. About Fred's dad, I mean."

Mekkam's red eyes went narrow, but his friendly expression didn't change. "He is one we do not speak of, Jonas. I do not expect you to understand all of our cultural—"

"Excuse me, sir," Fred interrupted, "but seeing as how it's *my* dad, I should have a say in what happens next, don't you think?"

A short, difficult silence followed her statement. Given how anxious she'd been to leave the closing walls of the URV just a few seconds ago, she couldn't believe she was finding an excuse to linger.

"Jonas can ask whatever he wants about my family," she finished, wondering if Mekkam could throw her into the clink, or whatever the Undersea Folk equivalent was.

"Uh, thanks, Fred. Anyway, King Mekkam, the thing is—how could Fred's dad hope to be king? If you have all your special king powers?"

Thomas's eyes were wide but he said nothing; Fred imagined he was going to suck all the information he could out of whatever Mekkam's response was. Not that she could blame him; she planned to do the same thing.

Mekkam was frowning, but it was thoughtful, not angry. "We know now that he could not have succeeded," he said carefully. "And not just because many of his 'followers' were still loyal to my family. Yes, I can find an individual subject if I focus on that person. Yes, I can direct the thoughts of the Pelagic and project them into other minds. But none of it is unconscious. I must focus. I don't—I can't—"

"Eavesdrop?" Thomas suggested.

"Exactly, yes! Eavesdrop! I cannot do that."

"So, does being the king give you extra special cool powers, or do your extra special cool powers make you the king?"

"All of my line can do as I do," Mekkam replied, still being careful. Fred had the sense that the king did not want a misunderstanding to spring up. "Because of that, we are the royal family. Fredrika's father felt our time was done."

"Was he a really strong telepath, too?"

"Indeed, yes," Mekkam replied simply. "He *could* eavesdrop. But he did not have the control my line has built over generations. He was all raw power and ambition. And that is why we are here, and he is not."

A slightly longer silence fell, broken by Jonas's, "Okeydokey. Thanks for clearing that up, sir."

"You are a curious species," the older man said, kindly enough. "You have done great things as a result."

"Well." Jonas puffed up a little. "What can I say? We've been kicking ass and taking names since—"

"Third grade," Fred interrupted. "I'm outta here, Artur's waiting for me."

"God fucking forbid His Royal Majesty be kept waiting," Thomas muttered.

"Play nice," Fred scolded, inwardly smirking. "You guys are staying here to plunder your DVD collection?"

"Indeed, yes!" Mekkam boomed.

"Oh, I am *so* out of here."

"Me, too," Jonas said. "Can I borrow a scuba tank to get me all the way back?"

"For God's sake. It's not *that* long a swim."

"Says Fishgirl!"

"Do not . . ." she said through gritted teeth, stripping out of the clothes Thomas had lent her—Jonas didn't care, Mekkam didn't notice, and Thomas was too busy grilling the king on his telepathy to pay attention to her now-nude state—"call me that. Ever again."

"You won't even care if I drown," Jonas said mournfully. "You'll just swim off and go have dinner with your handsome prince."

"He's not 'my' anything." She paused, and grinned evilly. "And yes, I'd leave you and go have dinner."

Twenty-seven

Cruelly outpacing Jonas, Fred was shaking the water out of her hair and walking up the beach less than five minutes later. To her surprise, Tennian and Rennan, the evil blue-headed Undersea Folk twins, were sitting on the beach (nude, but then, that was normal for her father's people), watching the horizon.

"Good evening, Fredrika," Tennian said to the sand.

"Hi, Tennian. Rennan."

He didn't answer, just kept squinting at the horizon. Fred was about to verbally humiliate him when Tennian's left elbow slammed into his side so hard, Fred actually heard a crack.

"Good evening," her brother managed, then slowly flopped over on his side and moaned into the sand.

"We look forward to hearing your testimony tomorrow," Tennian added, looking up and smiling shyly.

"Do you?"

"Also, His Highness, *our prince* . . ." This was followed by a glare at her writhing twin. ". . . is looking for you."

"Yeah, Mekkam—*your king*—already told me. Thanks. Nice to see you guys again."

"Do you—" Tennian cleared her throat and tried again. "Do you know where Thomas is?"

"The URV. He's picking out movies for the king to watch."

"Oh."

Fred knew it was a perfect time to leave. Rennan had shattered ribs and would think twice before snubbing her again. Artur was waiting. The king was out of her hair. Thomas was out of her hair. Tennian didn't have the courage to interrupt her king, so she didn't have to worry about what Tennian and Thomas were up to.

Perfect.

There would never be a better time to leave.

Never.

So: time to leave.

"Thomas wouldn't mind if you swam over," Fred said to Tennian, surrendering. "In fact, he'd be delighted to see you again."

"Oh, but he is meeting with the king. I couldn't—"

"What meeting? He's lending the king DVDs. Never mind what they are," she added as Tennian opened her mouth. "The point is, it's not official business. Go ahead."

Tennian had already leapt to her feet, showering her moaning twin with more sand. "Well. Perhaps I will. In the interest of—of—"

"Interspecies communication," Fred suggested, cursing herself for having a conscience.

"Exactly!" Tennian cried, then scampered toward the surf. At once she stopped and turned. "Oh. Rennan. Good-bye."

"Yeah, toodles," Fred told Rennan, who had slumped over like a beached manatee and just lay there, breathing hard.

And off Tennian went, to slobber all over Fred's boyfriend. Well. One of her boyfriends. Not that they'd decided on anything official, because they certainly—

"Little Rika?"

"Coming!" she called, and stepped over Rennan's body to run up the beach.

Twenty-eight

"I have something to show you."

That was all Artur had told her. Then he'd led her to the shore and they'd waded in until the water was up to their hips. Then they dove, shifting to their tail-form.

I've spent enough time in the water today, don't you think?

I think you complain to hear the sound of your own voice, Little Rika.

And I think you should blow your—

Here!

She looked . . . and nearly gasped. Artur had led her to what appeared to be a good half an acre of seaweed. The dark green contrasted beautifully with the bone-colored sand, and the vegetation went on and on and on.

He caught her by the hand and led her to it, and she picked a large leaf off a plant and cautiously nibbled it. Then, growing bolder, she stuffed the waxy, plump leaf in her mouth and chewed.

It tasted salty and green, like the seaweed that came wrapped around maki rolls in a Japanese restaurant. It was delicious!

She grazed contentedly for a good twenty minutes, hoping Artur wouldn't make any cruel observations as to her manatee-like behavior.

See? I knew you would like this. Even those of us who eat fish like this.

It's delicious. I could make a salad out of this stuff. A little olive oil, a little rice vinegar, some sesame seeds . . .

Only I could show you this.

You, or any marine botanist.

She heard him snort in her head, and she stuffed a last leaf in her maw. *Yum! Better than spending your evenings cracking open clams like a damn otter or something.*

Little Rika, when the Pelagic is over, I wish you to come home with me.

Whoa! That had come out of nowhere. She thought they were having salad, not discussing living arrangements. *Home, the Black Sea home? That home?*

Yes.

She thought about it and he let her; they both floated just above the seaweed spread. Finally: *I think that might cause you some problems, Artur.*

Ha! My people are slow to change, but they do change. Why do you think it has taken us so long to even meet on this subject, much less make a decision?

Tennian laid it all out for me. That if it wasn't for you, everybody'd be dissing me all the time.

But I am here, and I want you to be my princess. If you are my princess, no one would dare be "dissing" you.

That's a pretty poor reason to marry into the family. To get people to like me.

I do not presume to know your reasons, Little Rika. I only know my own. The entire twelve months I had to stay away, there was not a day I did not think of you and wish I could be with you. Did you not think of me?

He had swum up behind her and was holding her around the waist, where her belly met her scales. His big hands were stroking, stroking.

Yeah, I—I thought of you. And one other.

You do not need to answer me this moment. Or even this week. But I do not wish to return home without you, Little Rika. I understand it is much to ask. But I can give you much in return.

And my job . . . ?

You can apply your training for the betterment of our people. Yours and mine. And one day you will be their queen.

Eeeesh. I dunno, Artur. It's a lot—

Yes. He nuzzled the slope of her neck and she was having a hard time concentrating on what he was saying. Thinking. *And I offer a lot in return. Only say you will ponder my offer, Little Rika. That is all I require of you this night.*

Okay. I'll think about it. I promise I will.

Then all is well. Abruptly he released her, and she was actually disappointed. Usually he got gropey and then she punched him. That was their thing.

Maybe Artur was trying a different approach.

Scratch *maybe*, she thought, swimming after him. Definitely. Question was, what was she going to do?

She thought about it all the way back to shore.

Twenty-nine

𝕾

She and Artur were still shaking the seawater out of their hair, ankle deep in the surf, when she heard the resort van wheeze into the driveway.

Okay, that was weird. Everybody was here already. The staff had been dismissed. Thomas had promised them privacy. It was probably just a grocery drop-off . . . but at this time of night?

She turned to Artur. "Get lost. I'm not sure who's here."

"As you like, Little Rika. I already have what *I*

want." And with a devilish grin, he waded back into the surf, dived in, and vanished.

Fred trotted up to the pool, where any number of towels were still scattered. She started frantically grabbing and discarding towels.

Jonas, still dripping and panting from his swim back from the URV, was sprawled on a lounge chair. "What?" he groaned as Fred hurriedly started wrapping towels around her waist, chest, and hair. "I almost *died*, you know. I almost died!"

"Shut up, you didn't almost die. Help me."

"Help you with what?"

"We've got company, but I don't—"

"Jonas? Honey?"

Fred knew that voice. She *knew* that voice! She'd been hearing it for years and, these days, had been hearing it far more than she ever had before. Not just at work, but at dinners, in her apartment . . . and now here.

Oh, God, please not here.

"Jonas?"

Horrified, Fred and Jonas stared at each other, then in the direction of the voice.

And—yep, there she was. Staggering down the path with a suitcase the size of a hope chest. And it was probably stuffed with lab coats.

"Dr. Barb!" Fred nearly screamed.

Thirty

"What the hell is she doing here?" Fred hissed.

"Don't hit me!" Jonas shrieked, cowering away from her. "Or at least, not the face! I just had a cucumber mask treatment." He threw his arms across his face and staggered up from the lounge chair in one oddly graceful movement. Fred resisted the urge to hook her feet between his ankles and knock him over. "I didn't invite her, I swear! I only—"

"Told her where she could find you. Left detailed

instructions 'in case of emergency.' This is obviously some sort of repellent romantic surprise!"

"You don't have to make it sound like she brought the plague," he snapped back, cautiously lowering his arms. Dr. Barb was about ten yards away and gaining; Fred could hear the shorter woman puffing as she lugged the suitcase. They didn't have much time to finish their fight. "In fact, it's kind of sweet, her flying all the way out here to surprise me."

"Oh, it's very fucking sweet, it's fabulous, it's wonderful!"

"Just because you're threatened by the appearance of anyone's romantic commitment—"

"Oh, like I give a shit about that right now, and you know it!"

"Wait. What? I know you don't give a shit, or—"

She roared right over him. "Now not only do I have to watch my ass, all the Undersea Folk in the area have to be careful, too! And guess who's going to get the blame for this? God *damn* it!" She kicked a lawn chair into the pool.

"Stop your whining for two seconds and try to remember that everything isn't about *you*. The person who'll get blamed for this is me, which is fine, because I'm the one who's got it coming. Now quit with the temper tantrum, force a smile onto your stupid craggy gargoyle head, and make nice with my girlfriend and your boss!" Jonas forced the entire diatribe out in one hissed breath, then his face broke into a beatific smile, and he turned and spread his arms. "Honey pie! Sweetie! Oh my God, you have *no* idea what a surprise your little visit is!"

"Really?" Dr. Barb chirruped, dropping her hope chest—uh, luggage—and rushing into Jonas's embrace. "Really, you're not mad? I just got so lonely, and the NEA can take care of itself for a few days, and I thought it'd be fun to fly down and surprise you." Dr. Barb looked at Fred with anxious dark eyes. "I know your family reunion is private; Jonas and I will of course stay out of your way."

"Fam—uh, right, right. Yep. My family is . . . well, they're just insane about their privacy. Almost pathological. You probably won't see any of them the whole time you're here." *God willing.* "And how long *are* you here?"

"Only 'til the end of the week."

"Come on, I'll show you my hut. I'll help you unpack. Could take hours," he added over his shoulder, imparting a final "behave!" glare to Fred before they left.

Fred jumped into the pool to retrieve the lawn chair, then gave in to her tantrum and crumpled it up into a rough ball. She watched it sink into the deep end and only wished Jonas's mangled body was sinking beside it.

Thirty-one

"Artur, Artur!" She realized what she was doing, cursed her stupidity, waded in, ducked her head under, and called, *Artur!*

She listened hard, and heard nothing.

Artur! Hello? It's an emergency! Artur!

Still nothing. Well, shit. She wondered what her range was. King Mekkam's appeared to be limitless; obviously run-of-the-mill Undersea Folk had to be content with the equivalent of shouting in an empty room. Or maybe that was a hybrid thing. Maybe—

—ttle Rika.

What? Artur? Are you coming?

Yes, Little Rika. And she could feel him getting closer, coming into her range. Damn. She was almost getting the hang of this mermaid thing. *What ails you? Have you hurt yourself?*

No such luck. My boss is here!

Your . . . from the aquarium on land? The woman Jonas has taken to mate?

Yes! She saw him and realized she'd floated out over her head; he was swimming toward her with powerful strokes, strokes that gobbled the distance between them and made it look easy. *She flew out to surprise Jonas! So you've got to tell your dad, so he can warn everybody. Jonas will do his best to hole up with her in his hut, but she's got to eat, and I imagine she'll want to swim and sunbathe and, I don't know, work on my annual review.*

As you wish, Little Rika. He reached for her and she let him, actually submitted to a hug, to being held. *Why are you so distressed, dear one? My people are well used to hiding; your Dr. Barb will not know we are there, even if we swim right beside her. This is nothing new.*

It's just . . . this is private. The Pelagic is private. I made them accept Jonas, and your honor made you accept Thomas. Now Dr. Barb's here. It's turning into a mess, and it's all because of me.

My Rika, you are too strict with yourself, surely.

It's just hard enough to get people to talk to me after what my dad did; now everybody's going to know there's another biped at the Pelagic. Good old Fred: totally dependable for traitorous behavior.

Fredrika, that is not so. He hugged her again and stroked her back. You are tired, I think.

And you're condescending.

But you are tired, he teased. Only exhaustion would lead you to own problems that are not of your own making. You fret over things you cannot control, or change.

I've got a lot to fret over!

So you do. And now you must rest; tomorrow you have much to do. He clasped her hand and started swimming for shore. Come. I will take you back.

Be careful of your tail!

He actually rolled his eyes at her.

Fine, next time another stupid biped shows up at

your super secret meeting, I'm not saying a damned thing!

Oh, Little Rika. Do not tease.

One disadvantage swimming in fins had: she couldn't kick him with her tail.

Thirty-two

She'd actually fallen asleep. The last few days with no sleep—followed by the stress of the Pelagic, not to mention Artur's proposal, then the arrival of Dr. Barb, and her fight with Jonas—had fixed it so she was snoring by 9:30 p.m.

Which made it all the more annoying when someone started pounding on her door.

"G'way," she moaned into the pillow.

Whoever it was took that as an invitation, because her door opened and she remembered . . .

"Why did I give you a key to my room?"

"Because you've been in love with me since the third grade," Jonas promptly answered. "What? You were asleep? It's not even ten o'clock!"

"Shut up. Go away." Her air conditioner was clanking and wheezing in the corner, and she finally took pity on it and got up to shut it off. "Never mind; make yourself useful and open the windows." She yanked one open herself. "What are you doing in here, anyway? Shouldn't you be having sex?"

"Oh, please, I did it twice already. And may I add, each time with me is more fantastic than the last."

"I actually threw up a little bit in my mouth just now," Fred informed him.

"You don't fool me. You're just mad because you never got to try a slice of Jonas."

"There it goes again! At what point does 'throwing up in your mouth' become just 'throwing up'?" She crossed the room and spat in the bathroom sink.

"*Anyway*," Jonas sighed. "Barb's wiped from the trip, among other things." He wiggled his eyebrows. "She's taking a nap; we probably won't see her again until breakfast."

Fred realized: "Hey! I'm not speaking to you. We're in a fight, remember?"

"Sure, I remember, but the good news is, I've forgiven you."

"You've—!"

"I thought I'd dig you up and we'd go grab a few drinks at the bar. But you're being your usual antisocial self, I see."

"Mumph."

"Man, that Tennian gal—blue hair? Blue eyes? She is a *key*-uutie!"

Fred rubbed her eyes. Tennian. Right. Between Artur asking her to live with him in the Black Sea, and Dr. Barb showing up, she'd forgotten all about the blue-haired troublemaker. "Don't remind me."

"She and Thomas swam out of the surf a while ago and walked down the beach looking like something out of a travel poster, except she was naked."

"Shut up."

"And where'd you disappear to before supper, anyway?"

"You mean before my boss showed up at a secret mermaid meeting? Artur took me out." Literally.

"Oh ho! So you've finally picked!"

"I haven't picked anything. He took me out and Thomas likes anything with a tail."

Jonas flopped onto the end of her bed. "Me-ow! If you're jealous—"

"I'm not jealous! Just disgusted. I could be anybody, you know. Anybody at all. It's not me Thomas likes. It's mermaids."

"Right, that's why he saved your life last year."

"He did not! I would have healed up on my own."

Jonas let that pass; they both knew there was more to it than that. "Well, did you like your dinner with Artur?"

"Yeah, actually. He showed me—he reminded me that there are things on the planet that only he could show me. Or, only one of my father's people. As much as I may like Thomas—and I absolutely don't—if I stayed with a biped, I'd be closing down an entire part of my life."

"Nothing you're not used to," Jonas pointed out. "I don't mean to belittle the sacrifice, but if you stayed with, ahem, a biped, it's what you're used to, comfortable with."

"Yeah, but with Artur, I can have it all. Also, he asked me to marry him and be the princess of the Undersea Folk and, later, the queen."

Jonas actually froze in ecstasy; she knew that look. He was having a "tilt! overload!" moment, imagining himself in charge of a royal wedding.

"Princess Fred!"

"Shut up, I haven't said yes."

"Which means you haven't said no!" He jumped off her bed and bowed low. "Your Highness, is it your plan to make it a policy that all the women have to look as bedraggled as possible?"

She snorted, and threw a pillow at him. "Nothing official."

"Oh my God! Princess Fred! I can't stand it, I absolutely can't stand it." He was actually spinning in a circle, clutching his elbows and whinnying in ecstasy.

"You know, there's a reason most people think you're gay on casual acquaintance."

"Stop it. You'll have to get married on land, of course—no way am I going to a royal wedding in fins, or that tin can Thomas built. Plus, there's your mom to think of."

"Will you calm down? I haven't said yes. I've got other things to worry about—like avoiding your girlfriend. And what I'll say to the Pelagic tomorrow."

"Yeah, yeah." He waved her citizen's responsibilities away. "Who'd pick Thomas over a prince? No offense. He's a nice guy and all. And rich; that helps. And you guys have the same educational background, the same training. But he writes romance novels. Artur's the prince of the Black Sea!"

"I'm aware," she said dryly, "of what they both do."

"So hurry up and tell him yes, before he changes his mind and decides to pick another mermaid. There's (literally) plenty of them in the sea, you know. Frankly, I'm amazed he didn't come to his senses all last year . . ."

"Will you get out of here? I'd actually like to get some sleep before I try to convince five hundred people who hate me that I know what's best for them."

"Hey, Princess Di didn't have it easy, either," he said, backing out her door. "But she became an icon! Fred the icon! I can see it now."

"Great, Jonas."

Thirty-three

🐚

You all know our next speaker . . . or know of her. Her father was Kortrim, of whom many of us no longer speak. Her mother is the Lady Moon, who loved her and raised her as her own, even though she was a surface dweller.

What a nice backhanded compliment, Fred thought, the snarkiness helping soothe her jangled nerves. I'll be sure to let my mom know that she managed to not chop me up into sushi despite being a drooling psychopathic biped.

She is a child of both worlds . . . She has lived among

the surface dwellers all her life, but is also of our people.

In other words, neither fish nor fowl.

She has kindly agreed to join us and bring her unique perspective to our Pelagic. Fredrika, if you will come . . . ?

Fred slowly swam toward Mekkam. Unlike a courtroom, there wasn't a specific place to sit (float?) and give testimony. Instead, she approached Mekkam, knowing he would pick up her thoughts and share them with people all over the world.

She thought, not for the first time, that it was no fucking wonder he was king.

Hello. And thank you for that nice welcome, King Mekkam. Yes, my name is Fred. Dr. Fredrika Bimm, that is, which means I studied marine biology for many years. I . . . have an affinity for it, you might say.

No one actually laughed out loud, but she could sense an amused rustling. She saw Tennian sitting very close and nodded at her; the young mermaid nodded back and smiled. She probably meant it to be encouraging, and it would have been except for all those scary sharp teeth . . .

I've been thinking a lot about your decision. Our de-

cision, I guess. And I can honestly say I can see both sides of the issue.

That must be why an outlander has been given a chance to speak today, on such an august occasion.

A merman she didn't know, one about her size, was floating about ten yards to her left. He had hair the color of snow. His eyes were the same color; it was such a startling contrast to his pupils that he looked blind.

You do not wish to hear what she has to say, Dessican? Artur asked, seeming amiably interested.

It is not a question of what I wish. It is a question of what is right. Her line has not been welcome here for longer than I have been alive.

Must be why you're so freaking threatened by me, then, Fred thought to herself, amused. Dessican had a look she well recognized: young punk, biting off more than he knew. And unwilling to back down in front of everyone.

Do you think we are not aware of her line? Artur asked, still sounding almost bored. *That my father did not know, and take it into account?*

If all can be heard at a Pelagic, I can be, too. And I do not think the king—

What? Now Artur's tone was almost a lazy purr. *You do not think the king . . . what?*

Dessican seemed to realize that, though others might object to Fred's presence, none of *them* were speaking up. And it was because all could be heard at a Pelagic that Fred had been invited to speak at all.

Invited by the king.

I am not the only one who thinks this, Dessican began lamely, looking around the large group.

Indeed. Just the only one ill-mannered enough to question the king's logic, not to mention his personally invited guest. Are you quite through, Dessican?

There was a long silence, odd in a group of telepaths, and then Dessican lifted his proud white head. *I am finished.*

Fredrika, Artur said, courteously gesturing her forward.

Ah . . . right. Okay. Glad we got that out of the way. Actually, glad somebody brought it up. I mean, Dessican was right about one thing. It's on everybody's mind. What my father did.

She swam in a small circle, thinking. She could feel all the eyes on her and, even more, could feel the *minds* on her, bending in her direction, trying to pick up every word.

So let's talk about it. Me, I didn't know a thing about it until I got here. After the king invited me. *But no need to belabor that point. And I'll have to admit, I was really, really shocked. Not just because I couldn't believe somebody who supposedly gave me my smarts would do something so dumb . . .*

An amused rustling; Dessican actually laughed out loud, and Fred watched the stream of bubbles for a moment.

Not just that, but because I know Artur. I had met the king by then, too. I couldn't believe somebody who knew them would want to hurt them. Kill them.

And I couldn't believe my own father would try to do that. And for what? To try to take over. Try to be the boss of all the Undersea Folk.

We don't have kings where I come from; everybody votes for the person they want to be the leader. And some people, they'll run for the job of leader just for the thrill of the title. Just to be called the leader, not to be actually doing the job.

I think that's what my dad wanted. To be called king.

To be bowed to and respected, but not to actually look out for you guys.

And what I think about that is, I think he must have been an ungrateful, treacherous bastard. I think if he was here right now I'd gouge out his eyes and show them to him for daring to try to put hands on the king.

So that's where I stand on the whole "Fred's dad tried to take over the world" thing.

I just thought we might want to get that cleared up before we went any further.

There was another one of those rustling silences, and a lot of people looked at each other, then at her, then at each other. Finally, someone Fred couldn't see spoke up.

Fredrika, would you continue your testimony, please?

Someone else: *The question before the Pelagic: should the Undersea Folk claim this planet along with the bipeds, or not?*

Fred tried to gather her thoughts. She'd expected the crap about her dad to take up half the day. Boy, once these people made up their minds, that was it. Something to remember.

Right. To come out of the water closet, or not. Okay. *Okay. Well, as I was saying before, there are two sides to this question, and I—due to being raised by a surface dweller—I can see both of them.*

On the one hand, why shouldn't all of us—all of you—have the run of the planet? Why should you hide? I can say that as someone who can breathe underwater, I'd sure like to be myself all the time, not just when I'm with a couple of trusted friends, or my mother.

Several of the Air Breather contingent murmured approvingly; she saw at once that many more people were looking at her than had before. Despite Mekkam's warm welcome, despite Artur's stated intent, despite Dessican's scene, many of her father's people had seemed set on ignoring her.

Not anymore.

But on the other hand, bipeds are treacherous. There's an excellent chance a lot of you could end up in an aquarium. Or a research lab. Bipeds have a way of thinking anybody different isn't human, isn't real, and therefore they can do whatever they like. And if you don't believe me, try to find a Sioux or a Cherokee Indian and ask them. Those are the guys who used to think the planet was just as much theirs. As a scientist, I've seen firsthand what the bipeds can do to the planet.

So what to do?

I don't know. I wish I could tell you that if you all chose to show yourselves to the rest of the world, things would work out fine and you'd be able to go wherever you like, unmolested. But I've seen too much of the human condition to be dumb enough to make guarantees.

On the other hand, if you stay hidden, you've lost nothing.

Of course, you won't gain anything, either.

I guess I'm saying it's up to you. All of you. I'll help you if you decide to show yourselves to my mother's people. I'll do whatever I can, even if that means "coming out" myself. Because I can hardly stay in hiding if all of you are brave enough to show yourselves to the world.

I guess . . . I guess that's all I have to say.

Fred "stepped down," or whatever the Pelagic equivalent was. She simply backed off and took her place in the crowd. Mekkam stood stock-still in the currents, his eyes closed, and after a long moment he opened them and said, *Does anyone have any rebuttal to Fredrika's comments?*

I do. Meerna, the tiny black-haired mermaid, was swimming to Mekkam. *How can we believe anything that comes out of her mouth? She was raised by bipeds,* she admits it! And worse, she was fathered by he whose name we no longer speak. She could be leading us to treachery. It would not be the first time for her kin.

I don't need to be treacherous to fuck you up nine ways to Sunday, Meerna, darling, Fred thought sweetly. Anytime I wanted I could pull your head off and use your blood to make the sea that much saltier.

You see? She thinks like a biped; all her reactions are that of a surface dweller. She is unkind, and prone to violence.

She is also "she who would be my wife," Artur said, coming up on Mekkam's left flank. Do you dare question my judgment?

Meerna opened her mouth—odd, for a telepath—and then closed it. She was silent for a long moment, until . . . Highness, I do not.

Well, naturally, Fred realized. What else could she say? Chickenshit. At least have the courage of your convictions.

No, Meerna's got a point, Fred added, cursing herself once again for being burdened with a conscience. Why should you trust me? Not because of what my father did—*I never knew the guy, so he's not likely to influence my actions today. And not because of what I said about what my father did. I could have been lying. Meerna's right: You don't know me. Which is why I couldn't advocate one course of action over another; all I could do was lay out your choices. You shouldn't trust me, and that's fine. You need to make up your own minds.*

So there.

Who are you to call anyone names, Meerna? Tennian said, out like a shot from her spot off to the side. *Fredrika took your insult when she could have done much worse. She does not know our ways but she has taken our rudeness without complaint . . . when she has the ear of the prince himself!*

Darn right, Fred thought. *The ear and pretty much any other part of him I want.*

She could have made any of our lives difficult whenever she wished. And what did she do? Stood up in front of everyone and gave her honest opinion!

Take that!

But even that did not satisfy you, and I suspect there are things in your family's past that would explain that.

Shall we explore your dark corners, Meerna, or will you remember your manners, remember you are supposed to be superior to the surface dwellers?

I . . . meant no offense. This was a rather large lie, but Fred was feeling generous in her victory.

And God *damn* it if she wasn't getting kind of fond of Tennian. Girl wouldn't have said shit if she had a mouthful when they'd first met, but now . . .

That's all right, Fred said. *It's the elephant in the room. We were bound to trip over it sooner or later.* If she'd been speaking out loud, likely none of them would have had the vaguest idea what she was talking about. But they plucked her meaning from her thoughts, and many people were nodding.

Anyway, I guess that's all I've got to say.

Before she could pull away, or scream, Tennian had seized her hand and was pulling her over to a large knot of Undersea Folk, all of whom had much friendlier expressions on their faces than they'd had twenty minutes ago.

Damn, Tennian, remind me to never get on your bad side.

Small-minded, close-minded, tiny-brained fools, Tennian was muttering, a constant stream of insults that flowed across Fred's brain. *As if we must be judged by the actions of one we had never met! Foolish, foolish . . .*

All right, calm down. Pay attention. Here comes more testimony.

The daughter of the surface dweller is right! an obvious Air Breather testified. *It is our land, just as it is theirs. Why should we hide? We have done nothing wrong! Why must we languish in brackish pools and never feel the sun?*

The Air Breather—Fred hadn't caught her name—went on in this vein for some time. Fred was amused to realize that when she'd heard "the daughter of the surface dweller is right!" she'd had no idea what the gal was going to argue until she'd said it. Because Fred hadn't really advocated either course of action.

This was made clear when several Traditionals spoke, also backing Fred up: we don't know how the bipeds will react; we can't trust them; it's safer to stay hidden as we have for centuries; we risk nothing and we lose nothing.

Oh, nuts.

What? Tennian sent back.

I don't think I've helped them resolve a damn thing.

Never mind. You did your job, which is all anyone could ask of you.

Then why did she feel like she'd let both parties down?

Thirty-four

Mekkam had asked Fred to remain after the Pelagic, so it was startling to see hundreds of Undersea Folk swimming off all at once . . . except for her. Several of them nodded to her, and one or two of the younger ones even waved.

Finally, they were alone . . . as alone as a mermaid and a king can be in an ocean teeming with life, anyway.

What can I do for you, Mekkam?

Only this. You were wise to commit to neither faction, but would you tell me your true thoughts.

If they'd been walking they would have fallen into step together; instead, she swam on his left, noticing he set a pace she could easily keep up with. Tactful, and then some.

That's just it, Mekkam. I really don't *know what you guys should do. I'd be fine whatever you picked. There's pros and cons to both.*

Indeed.

But you *must have a preference. Duh, of course you have a preference. In fact, the Traditionals are totally in your corner. You want to keep your people safe and I can respect that.*

But at what cost, Fredrika? To deny them their birthright? Smothering is not protecting, and I would rather not hurt my people while trying to help them.

Fred swam in silence for a moment. *Yeah, well, good luck with all of* that.

Would you really change your life if the Air Breathers swing the vote?

Sure. If all you guys will, it's the least I can do. Hell, all I'd have to do is show my boss my tail. It'd be all over Boston in a week.

That does not surprise me, since you would be

changing your life a great deal should you come with us. I am pleased my son has chosen well. Mekkam smiled at her, keeping his sharp teeth well concealed, and Fred almost smiled back. *I hope you choose him as well.*

Well, we'll see what we'll see, I s'pose.

That we will, Fredrika.

They swam back to the beach, both lost in their own thoughts.

For her own part, Fred was thinking that if her mother hadn't remarried, she'd have introduced Moon to the king.

What's wrong with me? she thought, horrified. Being around Jonas has given me matchmaking on the brain!

Thirty-five

§

"Great," Fred muttered as she stood up out of the surf, Mekkam beside her. "Here comes my boss."

"Hello, Dr. Bimm! Hello . . . er . . ." Dr. Barb, clad in a navy blue one-piece and an absurdly floppy straw hat, skidded to a halt in front of Mekkam. "You must be one of Dr. Bimm's family. I, ah, apologize for intruding . . ."

"No need, good lady. I am—"

"A nudist!" Fred burst out. "We're all . . . I mean, my

family is all nudists. We like to be nude. All the time. That's why the private resort."

"Of—of course. I understand. I—I'm making you uncomfortable and I apologize. I'll—"

"Not at all, good lady. Will you dine with us? I would like to hear more about the New England Aquarium. Fredrika and I will clothe ourselves, of course."

"Of course," Fred added sourly.

Mekkam gallantly held out an arm. And without so much as a half second of hesitation, Dr. Barb latched on to it.

No doubt about it, Fred thought, trudging behind him. The old guy's still got it. Wouldn't Dr. Barb shit if she knew how old he was, never mind what he *really* looked like when he was naked?

"I think it's wonderful that your whole family can get together like this."

Mekkam forked another lobster claw onto Barb's plate. "Oh, we do not do it very often, good lady. This is a special occasion."

"I gathered. Dr. Bimm has never had a vacation in all

the years she has worked for me, and then all of a sudden she took all her accumulated time at once!"

"The islands beckoned," Fred said sourly, polishing off another biscuit.

"We have much family business to discuss," Mekkam continued, refilling Dr. Barb's iced tea. "Perhaps we will need your help with some of it."

"And perhaps not," Fred said sharply.

"Oh, I couldn't presume to interfere," Dr. Barb said seriously. "It's bad enough I'm here at all."

Jonas kicked Fred under the table before she could form a suitably acidic reply.

Mekkam smiled, but it was an odd look: distant and almost unfriendly. "You never can tell," he said. "All things come together in the end, whether we wish it or not. Some might see your arrival here as a portent."

"And some might see it as a pain in my— Owwww, Jonas!"

"Sorry. My foot slipped again."

"My *fist* is going to slip if you don't cut the shit!"

"Fredrika," Mekkam said with absent authority. "Jonas. You have attained maturity; display it for us, if you please."

Embarrassed, Fred and Jonas stopped in mid-squabble. Dr. Barb's eyes went wide and, when Mekkam went out to see Artur, she leaned over and whispered, "He's the patriarch, isn't he? Your uncle, maybe?"

"Patriarch, yeah," Fred sighed. "Something like that."

Thirty-six

"Oh my God! It's after me! It's gonna kill me!" Jonas was frantically thrashing his way back to her. His snorkel was askew and his mask was on crooked as he sputtered and flailed. "Get it away. Get it awaaaaaay!"

Fred saw the ray, a gorgeous specimen with a four-foot wingspan, and swallowed a sneer of disgust. "Will you calm down? It's harmless."

"Tell that to Steve Irwin," Jonas retorted. "God, I'm surrounded by living creatures! This sucks!"

"Well, it *is* the ocean, Jonas. And stop thrashing.

You're doing a perfect imitation of a nice plump seal in distress."

"Aaagggghhh!"

"Oh, calm down. You're perfectly safe. We're not even thirty feet offshore." Dr. Barb was still sunbathing on her stomach, Fred was relieved to see, and there was no chance she could see Fred's tail, even if she was facing the right way and staring straight at them.

"That thing is huge!" Jonas accidentally took a gulp of salt water and coughed for five minutes. "I'm telling you, it's thinking about how I might taste."

The ray couldn't have given a shit about how Jonas might taste; it was swimming gracefully around them, either curious or looking for food or both.

She tried to distract him. "Hey, you know what another name for a ray is? Mermaid's purse!"

"How fascinating, now will you please kill it so that I may live?"

"I'm not killing it, Jonas." She grasped his arm, peeked again at the dozing Dr. Barb, and with a powerful flex of her tail, propelled them twenty feet in the other direction. "There, okay? Now you're surrounded by just fish and maybe a sea turtle."

Jonas coughed for another ten minutes. "You want to warn me before you turn the motor on?" he gasped after a long while.

"All you've done since we've gotten to this island is bitch. Well, that and have sex with Dr. Barb. What's the matter?"

"Are you kidding? You don't think it's a little stressful, spending all day on the beach wondering what you guys are talking about? Then worrying your girlfriend will figure out your best friend's biggest secret?"

"Lame," Fred decided.

"Drinking rum and Cokes all by yourself because your girlfriend is a scientist who just *has* to go poking around the local flora and fauna? She spent three *hours* feeding grapes to the iguanas yesterday—"

"Poor baby. Even when she's here, you're feeling ignored."

"—wondering if today's the day you're going to decide to beach yourselves all at once, preferably in front of CNN cameras? Do you know how stressful that is?"

"*You're* stressed? I've been freaking out ever since I found out my testimony might actually have an *impact* on the decision!"

A long, dark shape glided past Jonas, and Fred couldn't help it; her eyes widened. Unfortunately Jonas saw and spun around. "What? What? Oh my God, it's a great white, isn't it? *Isn't it?*"

"Could be," Fred said cautiously. "I don't think I can take one on by myself. Just . . . sit . . . still . . ." *I'm going to hell,* she reminded herself with an internal grin.

"Oh my God!" Jonas screamed in a whisper.

The dark shape surfaced . . . and blew a stream of water between Jonas's eyes. "Good evening, Jonas. Little Rika."

"You scared the hell out of me!" Jonas roared. "Don't ever do that again unless you want to be chopped into a hundred Filet-O-Fish sandwiches! I know the VP of marketing at McDonald's; I could make it happen!"

"Jonas is feeling a little hysterical this evening," Fred explained. "I think he's having his period."

"I did not know such things were normal for the males of your kind."

"They aren't," Jonas huffed. "I'm out of here. You two will have to find some other biped to torture." He began laboriously paddling toward shore. "And you both have split ends!" was his parting shot as a wave closed over his head, swallowing the rest of his insults.

"I didn't really think about it like that," Fred said, watching him go.

"Like what, Little Rika?"

"He said it's really nerve-racking, waiting to see what we decide."

"For us no less than him."

"Right, right. What's up?"

"Nothing is up." He pulled her into his embrace and nuzzled the top of her head. "I only wished to see you."

"Oh. Well, that's nice. Careful, Dr. Barb's onshore."

"I see her. Though I seriously doubt she sees me . . . or you, for that matter." He dismissed Dr. Barb with a shrug. "You did well today. I expected nothing less, of course."

"Of course. Well, it was definitely interesting. Never thought I'd see Tennian riding to the rescue, that's for sure."

"Yes, she is something of—you would call her a rebel."

"Tennian?"

"Oh, yes. She was the despair of her family for many years."

Fred started giggling and was afraid she wouldn't be

able to stop. "Oh, right. I can see it now. They must have wept over her antics for days. Months!"

"Are you quite well, Little Rika? You seem in . . . unusually high spirits."

"I'm probably light-headed," she admitted. "Haven't had a chance to eat today."

"Then come along."

"Oh, more seaweed grazing?" she asked hopefully.

"If you wish."

"I really liked that place."

"As did I, and not only because you were pleased to join me."

"Artur, what if I have to tell you no?"

The smile slipped from his face. "I will have to devoutly hope you do not."

"But what will you do? Find someone else?"

"Ah, Little Rika. Were you not listening to your own testimony? There is no one else like you."

"How horrifying," she joked.

"But singularly comforting," he said, and leaned forward, and kissed her softly.

She kissed him back, and the waves rocked them, pushing them farther into each other's embrace.

"Rika, my Rika . . ."

"Not your Rika," she mumbled against his mouth. "Don't spoil this."

"Oh, never! Tell me, Rika, are you fertile?"

"You mean, right this second? No. But in general? Yeah. I'm pretty sure." She menstruated, which had to count for something. She assumed she was fertile because she had not had occasion to think otherwise. Funny how her own biology was of no interest to her at all.

But maybe that was just another way to hide.

"Oh, excellent."

"If your plan is to knock me up and force a shotgun marriage," she warned him, "it won't work."

"The thought," he assured her, nibbling an earlobe, "never crossed my mind."

Thirty-seven

Good morning.

Hi.

Hello.

Morning.

Good morning, Fredrika.

Hi, Tennian.

This is my friend, Bettan—I believe you met?

Sure. Fred shook hands with the lean, red-haired mermaid.

I hope you will not judge me by the company I keep,

Bettan teased, no doubt referring to Meerna's anti-half-breed diatribe from yesterday.

Gosh, that would be terrible! Being judged by the people you're with instead of, you know . . . who you are.

An awkward silence followed that, and Fred had a rare twinge of conscience: had she gone too far?

But then Tennian, as usual, saved the day. *You are wise, Fredrika, as well as fearless. And yes, that would be terrible.*

I found your testimony quite interesting, a strange merman she'd never met spoke up in her mind.

As did I, a merman named Linnen added.

They chatted for a few minutes, Fred well aware she had Tennian's outburst the day before to thank for everyone's friendliness. And Artur, of course.

When the group broke up, Tennian whispered in her brain, *What's amazing is, Linnen is a Traditional and Coykinda is an Air Breather! And yet they both found something to take away from your testimony.*

In other words, I didn't help at all: things are exactly the way they were two days ago.

Someone with a grim view of things might see it that way, Tennian admitted.

That's me, baby. Grim View is my middle name. Well, names. Say, Tennian, can I ask you something?

Ask.

Which are you?

Oh, I'm an Air Breather! I do not wish to hide!

Fred snickered. *Why am I not surprised?*

But my family is Traditional. They think it is dangerous to expose themselves to the bipeds. And they side with the royal family in all things.

Not you, though, huh?

Artur understands, Tennian thought confidently. *We were babies together.*

Well, your family's not entirely wrong. It might be dangerous.

So is swimming alone in strange water; so is hunting in killer whale territory. Life is dangerous, and I do not care! It would be worth it to walk on the grass and not be afraid all the time.

If you break out into a rendition of "Part of Your World" I'm going to beat you to death.

Eh? Oh, see! It starts.

She was right; it did.

They will lock us up in their aquariums! Fredrika is

right: they will use their knives on us to explore our bodies, and never once think they are hurting people who are as they are.

And:

Fredrika is right! The planet belongs no more to them than it does to us; we have as much right to a beach house as a—a—

Hollywood film producer, Fred added helpfully.

And:

The traitor's daughter is right! Her people foul the water; they will not respect our rights. Better to stay hidden.

That is not what the traitor's daughter is saying!

Uh, guys? The name's Fred, okay?

And:

We will never agree; I do not understand why King Mekkam has not called the question.

It has not been so very long; do you imply we are as the surface dwellers, never agreeing on anything?

Ask Fredrika; she would know. I do not. I only know I will not change my mind.

Nor will I!

Very well, then!

Yes, very well!

Fred rubbed her temples. Around her, testimony went on while minor arguments broke out on all sides. Mekkam called the place to order again and again, but chaos lurked. She wished for an Advil. She wished for a bottle of Advil.

Finally, the day's testimony was over. But this time, she was followed—chased, really—back to shore by several Traditionals and Air Breathers, all interrupting each other to be heard on the issue, all waiting for her to validate their opinions.

Guys—

Surely you can agree that the history of your mother's people speaks for itself.

Guys, I'm really—

Data does not speak for itself! Fredrika would tell you that her mother's people have goodness in them, too.

Guys, it's been a really long day.

Fredrika could use her science powers to protect us! She would not allow her father's people to be enslaved.

Guys, I've got a splitting headache.

Fredrika is only one person; how can she stand against millions?

A familiar silver orb floated into sight and Fred arrowed toward it so fast, she nearly knocked herself unconscious on a viewing window. She pounded on the plastic until the air lock slid open.

Later, guys. She gave the chattering mermaids a hurried wave, and darted into the URV with pure gratitude.

Thirty-eight

🐚

"They're after me, Thomas, they're after me!"

"Fred, calm down." Thomas handed her a towel, and a robe. He waved at the Undersea Folk who were still milling around outside the URV. "Long day, huh?"

"You have *no* idea. I went from being totally ignored to totally harassed." She shrugged into the robe and toweled her hair dry. "God, and the voices! You just can't get them out of your head, no matter how hard you try."

"If I didn't know better, I'd be prescribing you some tranqs right now."

"I could use some, believe me." She slumped against the galley counter. "Got any booze in this thing?"

"That bad, huh?"

"It's just—that's a lot of people to have in your head, you know?" She looked out the window. "I'm used to having my brain to myself."

"Does it hurt? The telepathy?"

"Huh?" She jerked her attention back to Thomas, who handed her a beer. "Oh. No. No, it doesn't hurt at all. It's just overwhelming. Sometimes. Tell you what, I can see why exile is such a big deal to these people. If you grow up used to hearing all those voices . . . and then all of a sudden you're all alone . . . My father must have hated it."

"Your father sounds like a shitheel who had it coming," he said cheerfully.

"Well, yeah." She sipped her beer. "Boy, it's nice in here! Nice and quiet."

"Ah, my sinister scheme to get you alone has succeeded beyond my wildest dreams."

"Are you talking to me, or plotting your next romance novel?"

"Both," he said, and then kissed her spang on the mouth.

"Perv."

"Beer breath."

This time she kissed him, letting the towel drop from her hair as she put her arms around him, pressing against him as his arms came around her. She ran her fingers through his thick dark hair and stroked his teeth with the tip of her tongue.

"This is—what I'd call—a mixed signal," he gasped, coming up for air. "Usually now's the time you sock me in the eye."

"I'm really tired, though."

"Too tired to try out the bed?"

She laughed as he squeezed her to him. "I'm having an off moment as a result of a brain full of voices not my own, but I haven't taken total leave of my senses."

"Shit."

"Don't sulk," she teased. "You're hardly cute when you do that."

"Looking cute is the least of my problems," he growled, carefully setting her aside. "And stop doing that to my hair, it makes me feel like ripping that robe right off you."

"I see I'm not the only one under stress."

He went to a board of instruments, glanced at them without really seeing them, and closed the tiny door to the fridge which, in his distraction, he'd forgotten to do before.

"Not stress, exactly, but for a while there it looked kind of tense. As strong as you guys are, I'd hate to see you come to blows. Over anything."

"And they're even stronger than I am. No, nobody's coming to blows. But it's a charged issue, that's for damned sure. And I took the easy way out: I didn't pick a side."

"Yeah?"

She sighed and looked at her feet. "Yeah. Laid it out for them, pro and con, but didn't actually pick a side."

"Then came in here to hide."

"Pretty much, yeah. Dr. Barb's waiting for me on land, and those guys are all waiting for me the minute I swim out of here."

"Well, the URV's yours whenever you want it. I'm glad it's making a nice hidey-hole for you."

She quirked an eyebrow at him. "You wouldn't be calling me a chickenshit, would you, Doctor?"

"Not to your face," he replied, then laughed. "It wouldn't—uh-oh."

"What?"

She heard the click, and then the cycling of the air pump. "Great," she grumbled. "What now?"

She hit the button, and the door slid open to reveal, naturally, Jonas and Dr. Barb.

Thirty-nine

His scalp still sizzling from the glare Fred had given him as she and Thomas had left the URV, Jonas led Dr. Barb the few feet to the bedroom. Worth it, worth Fred's ire (which, frankly, he brought on himself at least twice a week) and then some, because he'd been positively—

"I've been *dying* to try this place out," he confided, while his lover looked around the small underwater RV, exclaiming and staring and, he could tell, wishing she'd brought her BlackBerry. "You know, the bedroom?"

"This thing is a wonder of design!" the scientist said,

momentarily elbowing the lover out of the picture. "It must have cost your friend a fortune!"

"Yeah, well, he's loaded and he can spare it, now check out this bed."

"And he's been living in it?"

"Yes. No. I don't know." Best not to get into the whole "No, just tools around during the Pelagic taking pictures" thing. "Barb, will you get your delectable ass over here?"

"And to think, it's all contained in—yeeek! Jonas!" She giggled and slapped his hand away, but he stood his ground and, as he outweighed her by a good thirty pounds of muscle, was easily able to drag her toward the small bedroom.

"Jonas, you act like you've been denied . . . Now just let me get a closer look at the design . . ."

"I *am* being denied." He started pulling on the straps of her swimsuit which, since they were wet, fought him like a live thing. "Right this second I'm being denied. Ack! What are you wearing, titanium?"

She laughed at him, brushed his hands away, then wriggled out of her suit with a few grunts, exposing much pink and cream flesh as she did so. Eventually (finally!), she was nude and holding out her arms. "There, Mr. Impatient, satisfied?"

"Not even close," he growled, then picked her up and tossed her on the small bed. His trunks were much easier to get rid of, and then he pounced on her.

"I really should be studying this thing's schematics," she told him between kisses.

"What 'thing' are you referring to?"

"After a year, you don't know?"

"Very funny." He kissed her mouth, the slope of her neck, the tops of her creamy, cool breasts.

"Oooh, your mouth is nice and warm," she groaned.

"I missed you so much."

"I missed you, too." She shifted her weight, pushing her nipple farther into his mouth. "I'm glad you liked my surprise."

He kissed, sucked, nibbled. "I loved your surprise. Adored it! It was the greatest surprise I ever got in my whole life!" He thought briefly of Fred and quailed, then banished the thought. The quickest way to lose his hard-on would be to think of his childhood friend—practically a sister to him!—in a murderous rage. "I loved seeing you, loved the surprise!"

"I just thought—since you were stuck down here—
with all of Fred's family—that you might like company."
Each time he kissed her she had to pause. "I know—you
like—to help her—in social situations—"

"I could use help in a social situation right now."

"Oh, yuck!"

They laughed together, as lovers will, and moved together, and kissed, and touched, and when he entered her
she moved against him like a wave, and clung to him.
And as her orgasm rippled through her she whispered in
his ear, told him she loved him, told him he was for her
and she was for him, whispered love, whispered, whispered.

Forty

Jonas groaned as the love of his life bounded off the small bed, cleaned herself up in the smaller bathroom, then wriggled back into her swimsuit. He had just enough energy to roll over and take a nap.

"Why does sex energize you like this? My God, you're acting like you had a Red Bull IV drip."

"Physiology, my love." Barb snapped her straps into place. "Now: your base needs have been taken care of, and nothing is going to stop me from examining this thing."

Jonas groped for his trunks, found the pocket string, found the small hard object tied securely to the string. "Hey, Barb."

"Jonas, I already told you—" .

"Be my wife?"

"—that nothing— What?"

He yanked, but he'd done too thorough a job tying the engagement ring to his trunks. "I want to get married. I think . . ." Yank, yank. ". . . we should get . . ." Yank! ". . . married."

Barb came over to the bed and after a final, futile yank, he presented her with his swim trunks. She did some sort of womanly thing and then the ring was free. "Oh, Jonas! It's a pearl!"

"From the ocean," he prompted the marine biologist.

"But—but you didn't know I was going to be here!"

"Are you kidding? I've been walking around with that thing every minute of every day for three weeks."

"For three weeks? Why did you—"

"Barb, is that a yes or a no?"

"What? Oh!" She slipped the ring on. "Yes, of course, yes."

"Really?" His postcoital lassitude vanished; he'd

hoped she was going to say yes, but hadn't been one hundred percent sure. She had, after all, been married before. "You will?"

"Oh, sure, I've been waiting for you to ask." She smiled down at the ring. "This isn't going to make Dr. Bimm very happy."

"Yeah, well—"

"Wait until she sees the pink bridesmaid gown I'm going to make her wear!"

Jonas gaped at his betrothed. "You . . . are . . . *evil*!"

"Yeah," Dr. Barb said, and giggled.

Forty-one

🐟

All morning, Fred couldn't shake the feeling that something was hideously wrong. Something had happened, she was sure of it. Something that directly affected her in a negative way. Something repugnant and bloated, just off the horizon. Something waiting to eclipse her life.

She was so busy trying to figure it out, she barely paid attention to Pelagic testimony. And for hours she'd half-listened to Air Breathers elegantly savage Traditionals, and vice versa.

This was essentially a playback of the last three days, she figured. It was like any emotionally charged debate . . . abortion, politics, religion. You'll never change the other person's mind. Never.

And what was *wrong*? Why the feeling of foreboding? She felt like Custer . . . the day *after* the Indians landed.

About three hours later, after a Traditional stepped down, Mekkam stepped up.

I've just received word. Enough of our people have heard testimony; they wish to vote. In the tradition of the Pelagic, the royal family will abide by the vote, regardless of the outcome. As will we all. Voting will take place at once; I will let you know when we have a tally.

And that was that. Fred suddenly wished she'd been paying a bit more attention.

Forty-two

"So that's it?"

"That's it," Fred said. She, Jonas, Thomas, Tennian, and Artur were eating in the small dining room. Tennian, she couldn't help notice, had put away enough shrimp to repopulate two fisheries. "They'll vote, and Mekkam will tell us who won."

"Uh . . . don't take this the wrong way, Artur . . ." Jonas began.

"I have noticed that when a biped says that, something offensive will invariably follow."

"Well, maybe." Jonas cleared his throat and put his fork down. "Anyway, Mekkam is the super telepath, right? It's why he's king?"

Tennian, Artur, and Fred nodded in unison.

"And everybody's—what? Beaming their thoughts at him? Until enough of them vote?"

More nods.

"Well. Uh. You said he's a Traditional. What's to stop him from just *telling* you what the vote is? From telling you the Traditionals won?"

"You think of our king as you are used to thinking of your own leaders," Artur said, mildly enough. Fred knew enough now about her father's people to realize Artur was being quite self-restrained. Especially given that Jonas had just insulted the hell out of Artur's dad. "But our king would not lie for his people. That would—ah—would—"

"Pervert," Fred suggested.

"—pervert the whole system of the Pelagic."

"Oh. Well, thanks for answering my question. I don't know that I'd have that kind of self-control. I mean, if I really thought staying hidden would be best for my people, I'd be tempted to just tell them that's how the vote went."

"Well," Artur said reasonably, "that is why you are not a king."

"And thank God. I've got enough headaches keeping track of *one* mermaid, never mind eighty zillion of them."

"Har, har," Fred said sourly.

"How long until the returns come back, so to speak?" Thomas asked. He slid the bowl of shrimp cocktail closer to Tennian who, Fred noticed with rising nausea, was eating the tails, too. She tried to ignore the crunching. "Couple of days?"

"The last time the Pelagic voted, it took about a day. It all depends on how many of us vote."

"Well, I'd think you all would!" Jonas cried. "It affects all of you, doesn't it?"

"Do all of your countrymen vote in every election?" Artur asked.

"Yeah, good point, but you're supposed to be better than us. You guys don't have any Republicans, at least."

"Oh, don't even start," Fred snapped.

"Well, did they wreck the country or didn't they?"

"They absolutely did not." Fred jabbed her butter knife in Jonas's general direction. "If we left it up to you

Dems, all the lifers would be out on the street and our taxes would be in the eightieth percentile."

"Like you even know what paying taxes is . . . you've worked for nonprofits your whole life!"

"I pay taxes," she said hotly.

"Yeah, for fun! The only reason you're talking like this is because Moon and Sam are rich. It's true," he told Artur and Tennian. "Fred's folks have more money than the Kennedys."

"Who are the—"

"They do not! And shut up. And—oh, shit. Here comes Dr. Barb." She checked; everybody had shorts on; Tennian was floating around in what she suspected was one of Thomas's T-shirts. "Watch the mermaid talk, you guys. And Tennian, will you stop *crunching*?"

"But they're so good," she replied in a small, wounded voice.

"Hello!" Dr. Barb trilled. She stopped short of the table and looked at Jonas. "Did you tell her?"

Jonas shook his head. "I was waiting for you."

"Tell me what?" Fred asked suspiciously, the feeling of foreboding back in the front of her brain.

Dr. Barb thrust her fist at Fred's face; she ducked. Then realized . . . "That . . . looks like . . . an engagement ring."

"Good work . . . Doctor . . . Bimm . . ."

"Oh, are you formalizing your mating?" Tennian asked, sneaking more shrimp onto her plate. "Congratulations."

"No!" Fred screamed. "You can't! Think of what it'll do to my personal and professional life!"

"There was that," Jonas admitted, "but aside from those benefits, we're also in love."

"Aw, fuck." Fred slumped over her plate and hid her face. "By which I mean, congrats."

"Thank you," Dr. Barb said. To Jonas: "That went much better than I expected."

"Believe it or not, Dr. Barb, I actually have bigger problems than this right now."

"Family reunions can be stressful," her boss said sympathetically.

There was a furtive crunch and Tennian looked guilty as Fred glared at her. "Tennian, please! Stop eating the tails!"

"You should not treat her so, when she does such a good job standing up for *you*. As, of course, do I," Artur added without a trace of braggadocio.

Trying to stomp on her rising hysteria, Fred managed not to yell, "Well, I don't need your help, or her help, or anybody's help!"

"Oh, here we go," Jonas said to his peas.

"No, it's not the usual independent rant. It's the 'I deserve to be heard based on who I am, not who my father is' rant. I can't believe I actually had to *say* that. I'm not the one in the wrong; your people are! In fact, I—I—"

She stopped talking, startled.

"Fred?"

Why hadn't she thought of it before?

"Fred?"

It was so simple! Why hadn't any of *them* thought of it before?

"Fred!"

She grabbed Artur by the collar (for a wonder, he was wearing a shirt, too). "Quick! Where's your dad?"

Forty-three

Little Rika, I must warn you, he is likely in meditation. It is exhausting, catching all the votes with his mind like this. He—

I don't care. I've got to talk to him. I've got it!

So you said, but you have not elaborated.

Bring me to the king, and I'll elaborate all you want. There.

She could see the king floating in about forty feet of water. He was upside down, his long grayish red hair almost dragging through the sand.

Mekkam! Excuse me? Mekkam?

He cracked one eye open and observed her. *Yes, Fredrika? Is something wrong?*

Yeah, you're going about this totally the wrong way!

The other eye slowly opened. *Indeed?*

Yeah. Uh. Sorry to interrupt. In her excitement, she darted around and around him. *Listen: it's wrong to make a group decision on something that will affect every single person differently.*

Oh?

She mentally gulped at the dry voice. And thought to herself, *I'm the only one who'll talk to the king like this. I've got to try!*

I think rather than forcing everyone to comply with the group vote, you let each one of your people make up his or her own mind.

But if, say, a third of them wish to expose themselves—

Where's the rule that says you all have to? In fact, let the Traditionals stay in hiding, if they want. That way the Air Breathers will always have a home to retreat to. You're not exposing everyone to one decision. You're not exposing people who want to stay safe.

Mekkam closed his eyes again and thought it over.

I do not know, Rika, Artur said worriedly. *We are a people of tradition, and by tradition the Pelagic—*

If you guys want to show up in the twenty-first century, you've got to act like it. And that includes chucking a legal system that's four hundred years old. Heck, ours is almost that old and it's a fucking mess!

Artur began, *I do not—*

Enough. I have decided.

Fred realized she wasn't too crazy about living in a monarchy. Why should one guy be able to decide something like this?

Then she thought, *One day it might be me making these decisions! Disaster!*

Fredrika makes a good point. Further, she has shown me a way to help all my people, regardless of which side they are on. How annoying not to have thought of it myself. But we are a prisoner of our own societies, whether we live in the sea or in the suburbs. It will be as she said.

It will? Fred gaped and was nearly spun away from him when she stopped paying attention and let the current grab her.

We will tell everyone. Right now.

And then, a moment later: *It is done.*

Forty-four

But how will we—
   Then I will return—
   —couldn't be simpler—
   —couldn't be worse—
And how can we—
But he said we could—
ENOUGH!

A hundred minds all shut up at once, and at least that many pairs of eyes were staring at Fred. She cleared her throat, remembered she didn't have to speak out loud, then added, *If you want to go up, go up. Just swim up to one of the public beaches and walk out. Or we could go hunt down the offices of* People *magazine. But one thing: Bipeds have a big-time nudity taboo. So if you want to hang out surface-side, you'd better love the idea of jeans and T-shirts.*

I will go. That thought, clear and cool, like a mountain spring. *I will go right now.*

Tennian. Shocker. Fred swam after her as she ignored the private beach and made for the public shore about five hundred yards away.

Uh, Tennian, they might be scared.

Who could be scared of me?

You'd be surprised. Just . . . no sudden moves, all right?

Fred could hear displaced water and looked; Thomas was chugging behind her and Tennian in the URV. She waved, then went back to following Tennian.

The blue-haired girl popped to the surface in full tail, a hundred yards offshore. There was a filthy boat staffed with sailors, all of whom started shouting and pointing at Tennian.

She waved.

Fred popped up beside her, squinting at the boat. There was something familiar about it, something she had read recently . . . it wasn't Navy, or Coast Guard. It wasn't a private yacht. It was—

"Pirates!" Fred gasped. Now she remembered, oh, yes. Modern pirates were popping up all over the place, robbing cruise ships and private yachts. "Tennian, don't—"

"Hello!" she cried, waving. Her tail was all too visible beneath the clear waves. "I am Tennian, of the Undersea Folk, wishing you—"

There was a crack, and Tennian disappeared beneath the waves.

Forty-five

🐎

Tennian!

I—don't— What happened?

Fred caught Tennian as she spun toward the sand bottom. Her blood was already darkening the water, which would bring the little guys: black tip reef sharks, white tip reef sharks, and grey reef sharks. They, in turn, would bring the big boys: makos, great whites, tiger sharks, hammerheads. Dammit!

You've been shot, Tennian. They shot you with a gun . . . a weapon.

But why?

Because they were scared of you.

But I did nothing!

Welcome to the wonderful world of bipeds.

She turned, feeling more displaced water, and saw Thomas had pulled the URV up right behind them, and was beckoning frantically toward her. And, like an answer to a prayer, Artur materialized on her other side and picked Tennian up out of the sand.

Come on, Thomas can fix this.

Do not be afraid, Tennian. Rika's Thomas is a most competent healer.

I'm NOT afraid. They were afraid of ME!

Fred saw a black tip reef shark circle toward them, waited for it to get closer, then punched it in the nose. It was either that or go for the eyes, and she didn't want to blind the fish for following its instincts. It spun away, sending a startled (and disgruntled) thought in her direction.

Three more came up on her blind side, but Artur bared his teeth at them and they darted away. In the ocean, she supposed the Undersea Folk were at the top of the food chain.

Remember where the boat was. We'll go back later and settle their hash, Fred thought.

Indeed. I look forward to that, Little Rika.

She saw a large shadow start toward them and thought it was probably a tiger shark. She started pushing and hurrying them along, never taking her gaze from the shadow. The three of them got through the air lock in record time, and then Artur was stretching Tennian out on the tile. Thomas had appeared, carrying a bulky first-aid kit.

"Finally. Took you guys long enough."

"Sharks," Fred said shortly.

"Great. Tennian, you doing okay, honey?"

"I did nothing!"

"Yeah, well, what can we say. We're a skittish and unpleasant race." Thomas pulled her into a half-sitting position and looked at her back. "A neat through and through. Probably a rifle. Did you see it, Fred?"

"It was long, that's all I saw."

"Rifle, then. Good. Small bullets," he told Tennian, "and not much damage. And they aimed high. Or hit high, anyway."

"That is good?"

"Very fuckin' good."

Blood was pooling beneath Tennian and Fred knew from experience that she had to be in pain, but the blue-haired mermaid only had eyes for Thomas, and seemed to hardly notice as he fixed her shoulder.

Déjà vu all over again, she thought. A year ago, she'd been on her back, bleeding like a pig and bitching to beat the band. Now . . .

Artur was looking at her strangely.

"What?"

"Can you not hear me, Little Rika?"

"Sure."

"I mean, before. Could you not hear me before?"

"Spit it out, Artur! What the hell are you talking about?"

"He said, 'This will not endear my people to yours,' " Tennian gasped. "You could not hear him?"

"Well, no. I guess my mer-telepathy only works when I'm in the water. Right?"

"Oh."

"You mean you guys can talk like that out of the water?"

"Of . . . of course. All of us can."

"Oh."

Artur and Tennian were looking at her with great sympathy, like she was missing a leg or something. "Who cares?" she asked impatiently. "Can we focus on getting Tennian fixed up, please?"

"Yes, of course," Artur said. He was having trouble meeting her gaze. "I was taken by surprise. I have never known anyone who could not—I mean, any Undersea Folk who could not—why, your *father* could—"

"Half-breed, Artur, remember? I didn't get the teeth, and I obviously didn't get the full ESP gene, either. Big fucking deal! Can we get back to Tennian now?"

"I am . . . well. I was just . . . surprised."

"Tennian, they *shot* you!"

"Yes. As I said. Surprised." She gasped as Thomas did something to her shoulder. "Very, very surprised."

"You got this?"

"I got it," Thomas said, not looking up.

"Then let's get up there and kick some pirate booty."

"I do not think that will be necessary," Artur said, but he followed her out the air lock anyway. And when Fred got to the surface, she got the surprise of her life.

So, she imagined, did the pirates.

Forty-six

The small, ugly boat was swarming with Undersea Folk. But the first thing to catch her attention was King Mekkam, who was holding the rifleman at arm's length and saying, "You do not harm one of my people without facing consequences, biped."

Two ladders hit the water and Fred scrambled up one. Artur was already on the ship. How did he *do* that? She saw three rifles on the deck, all of them with bent barrels. There were perhaps a dozen Undersea Folk and maybe eight pirates. No chance for the bipeds at all.

One of the Undersea Folk was Tennian's twin, who was standing on the captain's head. His teeth were being ground into the deck as he flailed and said, *"Mmmph gmmphh dmmmph!"*

"Oh, boy," Fred said. "So much for good race relations."

"They are thieves and law flouters, yes?" the king asked.

"Yes, Mekkam."

"Then we will turn them over to the authorities. Are there many like this?"

"Kind of," she admitted. It was tough to admit that pirates were alive and well in the twenty-first century.

"Then we can be of assistance to your authorities. We will be good at that."

"I guess," she said respectfully, trying to ignore the begging and screaming. "But are you sure you want to? Tennian didn't do a damned thing."

"Exactly so," her twin, Rennan, said, actually jumping up and down on the pirate captain's head. "So we, too, will try for the surface world."

"This is all my fault," she said glumly, sitting beside two unconscious pirates. "Me and my whole 'democratic process' speech. Me and my shitty advice."

"On the contrary, Little Rika. You did warn us. Many times. And Tennian is grown, and able to make her own decisions."

She looked up at him, realizing . . . "I would have known what they were up to. You organized and led an attack with your dad, from the URV. You did it all with your telepathy while at the same time you were helping us with Tennian. And I didn't have a clue what was going on, because I'm mind blind when I don't have my tail."

"It seems that is so." Artur knelt beside her. "But I do not mind, Little Rika, truly. I was surprised, true. But your differences make you the delight you are to me. And if you do not mind, I do not mind."

"Oh, the one-eyed person in the country of the blind and all that, huh?"

"What?"

"Never mind. What now?"

"Now the others have decided they will—"

"Come!" Rennan cried, and quite a few of them dived off the bow of the ship, shifted to tails, and began swimming for the public beach, which was crowded (as could be expected this time of year).

"But what about the bad guys?"

"They will sleep."

Fred looked. Yup. Pirates were all unconscious. Only she and Artur were left, conscious, on the ship.

Fred got up off the deck and stared after the swimming Folk. All she could see were their heads bobbing in the surf. "Are they *still* going to the public beach?"

"We can be a stubborn, implacable people, Little Rika."

"Oh." She nibbled her lower lip. "I see. Kind of a knee-jerk 'they can't scare us off' type reaction."

"Exactly so."

Artur and Fred dove off the stern and swam after the other Undersea Folk. One by one, the Folk swam up to the beach, shifting from tail to legs in full view of at least two hundred tourists.

"Hello," Rennan was saying to a delighted little girl. "I am Rennan, of the Undersea Folk."

"Becky."

Biped and merman shook hands.

"Becky!" Mama wasn't happy at all, and came running over, jiggling everywhere in her too-tight black one-piece. "You get back here!"

"Hello, madam. I am Rennan."

His outstretched hand forced her to remember her manners; she hastily shook his hand.

"Did you see, Mom? He's a merman! He had a tail!"

"Are they shooting a movie around here?"

"No, madam. Come and meet my friends."

Fred watched, amazed, as tourist after tourist came down to the water, some trying to cover the Folk with towels, most amazed at the transformation. Only the children were unrestrainedly delighted.

"Wow," Fred said. She waved as Jonas screeched up to the beach in the resort van. "Never thought I'd see the day."

Jonas was now hopping up and down on the sand, shaking a fist at her.

"What is he screaming?" Artur asked.

"Oh, the usual. 'You didn't tell me.' 'You left without me.' Yak-yak-yak."

"He seems agitated. Even for Jonas."

"Hey, now he gets to go home and start planning his wedding."

"Ah, a noble goal."

"Speaking of which, where the hell is Dr. Barb?"

By now Jonas had hopped back in the van and driven right up on the beach, a huge no-no. Jonas hit the brakes as the passenger door opened and Dr. Barb jumped out.

"What's going on?" she cried. "Are you all right, Dr. Bimm? Did you see the pirates?"

Fred, still knee-deep in the surf, abruptly sat down.

"Dr. Bimm? Are you well?"

And shifted to her tail.

Dr. Barb stared down at her. At her tail. Blinked. Rubbed her forehead. Blinked faster. Meanwhile, Jonas came up and put his arm around her. "Anybody get hurt?" he asked quietly.

"Tennian. And all the pirates."

"Dr. Bimm."

"Yeah, Dr. Barb?"

"You're a mermaid."

"Yeah, Dr. Barb."

Dr. Barb was blinking so fast, Fred wondered if the

woman was going to have to sit down. "Then this," she said at last, "this explains all those late nights when you'd insist on feeding the fish on your own."

"Yeah."

"This explains rather a lot, actually."

"Okay."

"Including your hair."

"Yep."

"This isn't a family reunion, isn't it?"

"No, Dr. Barb."

"Okay. I just wanted to get that cleared up." Her boss knelt and tentatively put a hand on Fred's tail, where her left calf normally would have been. "Dr. Bimm . . . you're really quite beautiful."

"Thanks, Dr. Barb. You can go ahead and have a heart attack now."

"Oh, no." Dr. Barb was scanning the beach, taking in the tourists and the other Undersea Folk. "There's going to be far, far too much to do." She was absently patting Fred's tail. "This changes everything."

"Think so?"

"This is our prince," another Folk was saying. "Prince Artur, and our friend, Fredrika."

"Hi." Fred shifted to her legs, stood, and shook hands with a strange, chubby male tourist who hadn't used enough sunscreen on his bald head. "My name's Fred, and I'll be your mermaid today."

Forty-seven

Much later, she and Artur went back to the URV to check on Tennian, who was drinking her third Coke and chattering to Thomas.

"Ho, my prince! Fredrika!"

"Your twin's up there kicking ass and taking names."

"Yes, I have been following the events."

Right. That darned telepathy . . . In full-blooded Folk, it worked wherever they were, not just in the water.

Dammit. She'd never felt more like just a half in her entire life.

"And see! Thomas has healed me."

"Not quite," he cautioned. "I think you should take it easy for at least a day. I know Fred heals quickly, but I've never treated a non-hybrid before."

"Well, super," Fred muttered.

"I am grateful you were here," Tennian said.

"Oh, it was my pleasure. Really."

Fred watched the two of them stare into each other's eyes.

Dammit! That fucking Florence Nightingale syndrome! He'd fallen in love with Fred after patching her up, then left for a year. Now here he was, slobbering all over Tennian and making a damned fool of his damned self, dammit!

Well, she didn't care. She absolutely did not. In fact, it made things an awful lot easier. Yes, it did.

She turned to Artur and abruptly said, "I've decided. I'll come home with you. I might even marry you. But one thing at a time. First, a visit."

Artur yelped with delight and swept her up in a

rib-cracking hug. "Oh, Rika! You have made me very, very happy. I have so many things to show you!"

Fred submitted to the embrace, and couldn't help but notice that Thomas didn't look up. Not once.

Oh, well.

That was that, then.

Dammit.

Forty-eight

ʒ

"You guys, you guys!" Jonas was yowling and Fred, Artur, Thomas, and Tennian ran the last few steps to the bar.

Dr. Barb darted out of the main lodge and frantically beckoned. "Hurry, Dr. Bimm! Prince Artur! You're on again!"

They had the television above the bar tuned to CNN, where the stream informed them of stock prices, and the talking head was saying, "—actual mermaids!"

"Undersea Folk," Tennian corrected.

"You knew and you didn't tell me," Dr. Barb was saying reproachfully to Thomas. "I think as your supervisor I had a right to know." She raised an eyebrow at Fred. "And as *your* supervisor I definitely had a right to know."

"Tough nuts."

"Yes," the talking head was saying, "actual mermaids."

"Undersea Folk!" Tennian almost shouted.

"See, if you're already yelling at the TV, you're halfway to fitting into our world."

"No, it's not a new movie, and no, we're not pulling your 'tail.'"

The group groaned in unison.

"It seems several tourists in the Cayman Islands spotted these mermaids—and mermen!—and although the sightings have yet to be confirmed, too many statements sound alike to be easily dismissed. Whether it's true or not, one thing remains certain: it'll be a whale of a sea tale. I'm Margaret Bergman, CNN."

"That's it?" Fred practically screamed. "Tennian gets shot by pirates and you guys storm the beach like the kids took Normandy, and all CNN coughs up is that it's an unconfirmed sighting?"

"Hey, one thing at a time. I'm amazed they broadcast as much as they did. And one of you guys will stand still long enough for a confirmed sighting, I've got no doubt about that. But never mind all that junk." Jonas pointed a bony finger at her. "What's this crap I hear? You're taking off? You're not coming back?"

"Not right away. Dr. Barb can find someone else to feed the fish."

"Not someone with your unique qualifications," Dr. Barb protested.

But Fred recognized the look in her eye, in any researcher's eye, and figured it was just as well she wasn't headed straight back to the NEA. "And my mom vastly prefers your company to mine, anyway, Jonas. I'm just heading down to the Black Sea with Artur to find out a little more about my heritage."

"For how long?"

She shrugged.

"But—" Jonas glanced at Thomas, who was hand-feeding Tennian shrimp. "Oh. Never mind."

"It'll be fine."

Her friend gave her an odd look. "Will it?"

"Sure."

But deep down, she had no idea, and was as afraid to see Artur's home as she was anxious.

Because everything was different now, and she had to take responsibility for that. For these people. If that meant being the queen, then that's what it meant.

As for Thomas—

She'd never really liked him anyway.

"But what am I supposed to do in Boston with you gone?" Jonas was whining.

"Have sex with my boss? Whoops. Former boss."

Dr. Barb moaned. "I can't believe you're doing this to me. You work for me for *years*, you finally tell me about your heritage, and then you quit, all in the same day."

"I'm sorry that my being a mermaid is making things stressful. For *you*," Fred added pointedly.

"But you'll visit, right? You'll have to visit," Jonas pleaded. "You're my best man. So to speak."

"Sure, I'll visit." Fred was thinking of Ellie's file, snugly tucked into her desk drawer back in her Boston apartment. Sure, she'd visit. At least once. She needed to have a nice, long chat with Ellie's father.

"Let us tell my father the good news," Artur said, and she smiled—she didn't have to force it, for a change—took his hand, and fell into step beside him as they hurried toward his father.

The king was shaking salt water out of his hair, and beamed at them when he saw them.

This is my life now, Fred thought. *These are my people. Who's better equipped to help them with the transition than me?*

After what happened to Tennian, I couldn't just turn my back on them and go back to my boring, lonely life.

I've got to help them. I will help them. Even—

"—but that is wonderful!"

—even if it kills me.

Turn the page for a sneak peek at

Undead and Wed: A Honeymoon Story

MaryJanice Davidson's new novella,
included in her upcoming anthology
Dead Over Heels.

I was so excited to land at the airport in New York City (LaGuardia or the other one . . . I wasn't paying attention to the pilot's intercom ramblings) that I didn't even bother with the stairs leading from the private plane to the ground. I just jumped, putting one hand on the railing and vaulting over, my black Gucci pumps dangling from two fingers. Didn't even feel the shock in my knees.

This was not a trick I could have pulled off while I was alive.

At the head of the stairs, my husband (husband! bridegroom!) Sinclair, king of the vampires, shook out the *Wall Street Journal*, folded it, and scowled down at me.

"How completely indiscreet, Elizabeth."

"Aw, Cooper doesn't care."

"Didn't see a thing, mum," Cooper assured me in his adorable Irish accent. He wasn't our pilot, and this wasn't our plane. It was my best friend Jessica's. She'd lent it to us for our honeymoon, told us we could go wherever we wanted. Cooper had worked for Jessica for ten years and, as they say, knew where all the bodies were buried. "An' by the way, glad to see you're not dead. That was a nasty business a couple of springs back."

"Horrible practical joke," I said, referring to my firing, death, thirtieth birthday, and return from the grave as the long-foretold vampire queen. The people who *didn't* know I was a vampire either never knew I'd been killed, or thought it was a nasty trick thought up by my (late) evil stepmother. My friends and I did absolutely nothing to disabuse them of their silly-ass notions. "Really really bad taste. But it all worked out in the end."

Meanwhile, Sinclair was gliding down the steps like a beauty queen (all he lacked was the tiara and bouquet of roses . . . and the tearful wave), when I knew perfectly well he could step off the I.D.S. tower and not even rumple his tie.

"Try to contain yourself." He sighed, moving past me toward the waiting limo.

"But it's New York City! And we're married! And we're in New York!" I, the country mouse, ran after him in my bare feet. I was wearing a sky blue shirtdress, no stockings. Oh, and my wedding ring! Not to mention my non-cursed engagement ring. But that was a whole other story. "Don't you think it's going to be a blast?"

He muttered something that I, even with my super vampire hearing, couldn't catch. Probably just as well. Behind us, Cooper was calling, "See you in a week, mum! Sir!"

I flapped a wave over one shoulder and practically dived into the limo. (Fortunately, the door was being held open by the driver, a tall, lean, gorgeous black guy with cheekbones you could cut yourself on.) Sinclair got in on the other side and shook out his paper once again.

"The Grange Hotel?" the driver asked.

"Yes," Sinclair replied absently as his pants made the dreaded chirrup. He fished out his cell phone, flipped it open, and blinked at the screen.

I sunk back against the luxurious leather seats, halfway to full pout. "Don't even tell me. Tina called again."

"No matter where I am in the world," he reminded me mildly, "I still have business to attend to. And so do you."

"Dude! It's our honeymoon, all right? If that thing beeps at your pants one more time, I'm going to *eat* it, understand? Now shut the fucking phone, toss the fucking paper, and bask in our mutual love and joy, dammit!"

"I'm not sure *bask* is the verb I'd choose," he replied, but at least he put the phone away.

"Nice of Jess to arrange a limo," I commented, relieved to finally get a fraction of his attention. We'd been married for three whole days and I still couldn't believe it had really happened. Of course, according to my bridegroom, we'd been married since the first time we'd had sex. Don't even get me started. "It's not like her to throw her money around."

"Point." Sinclair frowned. With his dark good looks, dark suit, broad shoulders, and strong jaw, he looked formidable anyway; when he wasn't smiling it was almost frightening. "She's the least pretentious billionaire I've ever known."

"Well, it's her dad's money."

"Correction. He's dead. It's her money."

"I mean, she doesn't consider it hers. It's not like she earned it. Hey, I'm not putting her down, but that's the way it is: she didn't earn any of it. That's why she doesn't throw it around, and that's why she has a day job."

Sinclair just looked at me. He knew me well enough to know when I wasn't coughing up the whole story. But in this case, it was just a theory. And the theory was that because Jessica had so recently (like, last week) recovered from terminal cancer, she was giddily celebrating life. Including throwing planes and limos our way. God knew what was going on in the mansion back home in St. Paul while we were away.

Never mind. I didn't want to know.

Sinclair, bless his cold, dead heart, tossed the newspaper on the floor and moved over until he was sitting beside me. He gave me a long, sweet kiss and cuddled me into his side. "Now, Mrs. Sinclair—"

"I told you, I didn't take your name!"

"—what would you like to do first?"

"I want to check into the hotel and have nasty kinky sex. Oh, and then go see a Broadway show."

"Odd," my husband commented. "I've never been alternately intrigued and terrified."

"Oh, shut up. There're lots of good ones."

We discussed the pros and cons of live theater all the way to the hotel. Even though it was full dark, traffic was horrendous. And the *noise*. It sounded just as busy at ten o'clock at night as it would have during rush hour. And everything was open! It was unbelievable. New York City: the perfect tourist trap for vampires.

The limo driver pulled us right up to the front of the hotel, a forbidding stone building that looked like a transplanted castle. Sinclair helped me out (not that I needed it) while the driver shoved our luggage onto three bellboys.

Hand in hand, we swept into the lobby, me trying not to stare like I had cow shit on my heels, Sinclair looking perfectly at ease.

Finally, I thought, tightening my grip on his hand, a squeeze that would have broken the metacarpals of most people, *I get him to myself, and the Big Apple belongs to us.* The month leading up to the wedding had been a frightening, lonely time for me and I was very glad to be reunited with my husband. Shit, I was glad he'd made the wedding at all. And now we were here, and I was going to make the most of it. Bet your ass.

Sinclair slammed to a stop so suddenly, and so gracelessly, that I plowed right into his back. "What's wrong?" I said into the cloth of his suit.

He muttered something again, and I peeked around him. Lounging across from the registration desk, taking up two small tables in the bar area, were Jessica, her boyfriend Nick, Antonia (the werewolf), and her boyfriend, a vampire named Garrett.

"'Bout *time* you got here," Jessica said, and raised her Cosmo to me in a toast.

"Oh, fuck me," I groaned, surprised—but not in a good way.

"I don't see how we can fit that into the schedule now," my husband replied, looking more distressed than I've ever seen him.

New York Times Bestselling Author

MaryJanice
Davidson

SLEEPING WITH
THE FISHES

Fred is a mermaid. But stop right there. Whatever image you're thinking of right now, forget it. Fred is not blonde. She's not buxom. And she's definitely not perky. In fact, Fred can be downright cranky. And it doesn't help matters that her hair is ocean-colored.

Being a mermaid does help Fred when she works at the New England Aquarium. But needless to say, it's there that she gets involved in something fishy. Weird levels of toxins have been found in the local seawater. A gorgeous marine biologist wants her help investigating. So does her merperson ruler, the High Prince of the Black Sea. You'd think it would be easy for a mermaid to get to the bottom of things. Think again...

NOW AVAILABLE

penguin.com
AD-01527 8

New York Times Bestselling Author

MARYJANICE
DAVIDSON

UNDEAD AND UNEASY

Weddings are never easy. But when you're Vampire Queen Betsy Taylor, they can become downright deadly. In the days leading up to The Big Day, Vampire Queen Betsy Taylor seems to have a full house and the wedding guests have yet to arrive.

Cold feet are no surprise, especially with an undead groom. But when her groom, Sinclair, truly goes missing—and not just to avoid wedding preparations—along with most of her friends and loved ones, Betsy is frantic. Alone and afraid for the fate of everyone she loves, Betsy can't trust anyone as she tries to find them and whoever is behind all the disappearances. And what happens next will shake the foundation of the vampire world forever.

NOW AVAILABLE

penguin.com
AD-01527 9

Dangerous, immortal, and thirsting for blood.

Laurell K. Hamilton
the Anita Blake series

MaryJanice Davidson
the Undead series

Christine Feehan
the Dark series

Diane Whiteside
the Blood series

Charlaine Harris
the Sookie Stackhouse series

Erin McCarthy
the Vegas Vampires series

Don't miss the best in vampire fiction.

penguin.com
AD-01194